I0573750

The LOOK-ALIKE
Bride

KATHRYN BROCATO
Author of *The Counterfeit Cowgirl* and *Georgie's Heart*

CRIMSON
ROMANCE

F+W Media, Inc.

This edition published by
Crimson Romance
an imprint of F+W Media, Inc.
10151 Carver Road, Suite 200
Blue Ash, Ohio 45242
www.crimsonromance.com

Copyright © 2013 by Kathryn E. King

This is a work of fiction. Names, characters, corporations, institutions, organizations, events, or locales in this novel are either the product of the author's imagination or, if real, used fictitiously. The resemblance of any character to actual persons (living or dead) is entirely coincidental.

ISBN 10: 1-4405-7475-8
ISBN 13: 978-1-4405-7475-7
eISBN 10: 1-4405-7476-6
eISBN 13: 978-1-4405-7476-4

Cover art © iStock.com/MichaelBlackburn

To
Mrs. Octavia Taylor
Physical Education Teacher and Coach

at
Camden High School
Camden, Arkansas

and
Brenda Clark Gilcrease
My High School "Twin"

Prologue

When Leonie Daniel first realized someone was stalking her on her regular afternoon jog through a Houston park, she tried to ignore the figure slinking in her wake behind the shrubbery. After half an hour, she found the whole thing annoying.

"Stop following me," she ordered. "I have enough problems today without adding you."

Despite the lectures she gave herself, Leonie's heart melted when the stalker halted and gazed wistfully at her with hungry brown eyes.

"Go on." She stamped her running shoe on the cinder path for emphasis. "Believe me, you don't want my big sister after you. If you hook up with me, you're a target."

She didn't need another problem today, especially a problem with the long, pointed nose of a collie whose fur coat looked like the poor creature had stuck its paw into an electric socket.

"Oh, all right." She melted under his longing gaze. "I'll buy you a hamburger. Then it's off to home with you. Do you hear that?"

The dog's ragged tail waved slowly.

Leonie turned and jogged toward the park entrance, followed at a respectful distance by the mat of orange-and-white fur, to a hamburger stand just outside the wide, stone gateway. She didn't even question how the dog knew who, of all the joggers in the park that day, would give into his silent plea. She was an easy touch and dogs spotted her instantly.

She placed the order for one hamburger, plain, and a cup of water, no ice, conscious of the hopeful brown gaze fixed worshipfully on her from behind some forsythia bushes.

In a secluded nook amid a group of white-studded baby's breath bushes, Leonie unwrapped the hamburger, muttering to herself about wet-noodle spines. While she was a wimp when it came to dogs, she did still cherish hopes of standing up to her big sister.

"Look. Let's make a deal." She laid the unwrapped burger on the grass and pushed it forward. "Just because I happen to be between jobs, my sister thinks I can drop everything and come running to help her out."

The dog gulped down the burger in two bites, then wolfed down the bun.

"It isn't that I don't love her and want to help her," Leonie went on. "But how am I supposed to have a life of my own if I have to keep pretending I'm Zara?"

The dog licked the napkin in hopes of finding an escaped morsel and waved his ratty tail.

"More to the point, how am I ever going to meet somebody special if every man I date falls for Zara the minute he sees her?" She shrugged. "Not that I blame Zara. She doesn't flirt with them. It's just that she's so gorgeous and outgoing, men can't help themselves."

The collie sniffed the napkin again then fixed his hopeful brown gaze on Leonie's face once more.

"Take Roddy Hillister, for instance. I really thought we were an item until Zara visited last month. We were *lovers*, for Pete's sake."

The dog's tail waved twice.

"He hasn't called me since, except to ask for Zara's phone number—he likes me, but the minute he met Zara, he said he knew he'd met his soul mate."

The dog made a whining sound in his throat. Leonie took it for sympathy and offered the cup of water.

"I've got to cut the family ties, or I'll never meet somebody who will like me more than he likes Zara."

The dog's long, pink tongue lapped water until the cup was almost empty, and Leonie gave in. She had never in her life managed to resist rescuing an animal in trouble.

"So, what do you say we team up? I can use a fellow like you around the apartment. If I have a dog to take care of, she can't expect me to go running off and leave you."

The animal licked his chops and looked hopefully at her. Leonie looked back equally excited. Maybe Zara would think twice about separating a woman from her dog.

"So. Do we have a deal?"

The dog wagged his tail.

"Do you mind a name that implies toughness, a little hostility, and a lot of protective attitude?"

The tail wagged again.

"In that case, let's get a move on, Butch." Leonie stood. "We've got things to do."

Chapter 1

Suckered again, Leonie thought. Why did she even try?

She didn't know why she tried to evade her sister's requests. Probably it had something to do with her desire to assert her independence—for all the good it did. Leonie always resisted, and she always wound up doing what Zara wanted in the end. No doubt, her spinelessness had something to do with younger-sister syndrome.

That was why she stood in the big open living room of Zara's lakeside cabin amid a batch of suitcases carried in for her by two nondescript government agents, dressed as airport shuttle drivers. Then they saluted her as if she were some kind of important official, and swiftly left.

Her current job: Pretend to be Zara.

She had done it before, but never for longer than a few hours. However, this particular job involved a hefty paycheck, which Leonie admitted she needed, and one month of impersonating her sister in an area where no one knew Zara, except by sight. She had been assured the job was perfectly safe, merely a precaution in the unlikely case hostile entities checked on Zara's whereabouts.

"All I can say is, this had better be as safe as they promised," she grumbled.

Leonie studied the suitcases, interested in spite of knowing she'd probably be heartily bored within a week. Experience told her she wouldn't care for most of the clothing inside. Zara's taste in almost everything was totally different from hers. Still, she'd have fun being a secret agent who looked like a Barbie doll for a month.

"I'm a pushover," she told the scruffy collie at her side. "That's all there is to it. A marshmallow-filled pushover."

Butch shoved his long muzzle into her palm.

"A broke pushover, too, which is the only reason I'm doing this." She brooded a moment. "You'd think I'd know better by now. Roddy Hillister should have taught me a lesson."

For a moment, Leonie toyed with the thought that this might be the perfect opportunity to have a vacation romance. She had always dreamed of a lover who would be hers for a lifetime, but sometimes a woman had to take what she could get. Maybe she could use playing Zara for a month to her advantage and make one of the many men always chasing her sister happy.

"Then Zara can deal with the repercussions," she told the collie. "That would teach her."

The collie's tail waved gently, as if in commiseration. He had spent the previous evening visiting the vet and the groomer and had metamorphosed from a matted ball of fur into a recognizable collie despite his moth-eaten appearance.

The vet surmised the dog was about two years old and healthy, although severely neglected. He thought Butch had survived on his own by foraging through garbage cans until Leonie acquired him. Even though a groomer had spent three hours trying to untangle the dog's coat, Butch still resembled a ragged orange-and-white blanket.

"It's too bad I don't have a job already lined up." She scratched gently behind the dog's ears. "You may have to get a night job guarding warehouses to support us when this is over." Leonie bent to pick up one of the suitcases. "We may as well get unpacked. We have a *vacation* to enjoy, courtesy of Uncle Sam."

An entire month. Leonie couldn't get over it. Zara, who was an agent for an unnamed branch of the U.S. Government, showed no compunction about interrupting Leonie's quiet life as a high school health and physical education teacher and demanding that she serve her country.

"If I had wanted to serve my country," Leonie grumbled, glaring into the suitcase open on the bed, "I'd have joined the army. Just look at this stuff. I'll look like a bimbo."

She held up a silver party dress that would fit like a second skin. It was so short, Leonie wondered why anyone bothered to call it a dress. Leonie would hide in the restroom all evening if she dared to wear what looked to her like a silver camisole in public, but Zara would be a knockout in it.

Nonetheless, that was what Zara—and the United States—wanted Leonie to do. Her job for the next month or so was to visit every place Zara would if she was vacationing at an Arkansas lakeside cabin, and knock all observers' eyes out.

Leonie smiled. She might as well enjoy this to the fullest. When she returned to teaching, perhaps she'd have memories of this once-in-a-lifetime vacation that would last her for years.

"Not that anybody who really knows her would believe for one minute that I'm Zara," she told Butch as she hung the silver camisole in the closet. "Only Zara can carry off looking like a movie star and have a great time doing it."

She assessed herself in the dresser mirror. Zara looked back at her.

Inside of one day, Leonie's ash-blond hair was lightened to a spectacular silver blonde, her eyebrows reduced to a thin, well-brushed line, and her skin, from head to toe, artificially tanned with an expensive lotion. Leonie's blue eyes were actually a shade or two darker than Zara's, but people rarely noticed that small difference amidst all the glamour Zara, or Leonie dressed as Zara, projected.

The two sisters looked so much alike, anyone would have thought they were twins, although Leonie was actually two years younger. Zara was brassy and outgoing, the sister who had her shoulder-length, ash-blond hair dyed platinum, and dressed like a movie star. Leonie, on the other hand, preferred to practice her baseball swing or kick a soccer ball around while wearing loose-fitting, sturdy jeans and T-shirts she picked for their serviceability.

Even during childhood, everything Zara did was perfect, unlike Leonie who was a walking disaster: her science project got eaten by her new puppy; and her first bra underwent an elastic collapse when she was walking down the aisle to the family pew at church.

Zara was a cheerleader and was elected homecoming queen. She graduated near the top of her class though she rarely opened a book. Leonie, however, felt lucky to graduate and had to work for all her grades. She excelled in sports and track and was well liked, but nobody considered her popular. Even the boys Leonie dated really longed to date Zara.

Once Leonie tried getting a tan and bleaching her hair, only to find everyone mistook her for Zara. Moreover, she discovered she didn't like the attention she attracted. She lacked her sister's gift for repartee and was incapable of turning a man down without hurting his feelings forever. Thus, after two days, Leonie returned her hair to its original color and deep-sixed her contract with the tanning salon. Not even moving to Houston had helped because Zara visited regularly and met most of Leonie's dates.

This time, things would be different. This time, she *was* Zara—for an entire month, and by golly, she was going to enjoy it.

Leonie studied her reflection in the mirror. She was supposed to be noticeable, so that nameless individuals involved in anti-American activities would assume Zara was vacationing at her lakeside cabin rather than tracking and sabotaging their operations.

Great, Leonie thought. Attracting the attention of people who hated Americans and wanted to kill them was just the sort of thing she preferred to avoid. For that reason alone, she deserved every bit of fun she could derive from this "vacation."

However, there was no way she could stand Zara's taste in clothes for hours at a time, so she smuggled along a tiny selection from her own wardrobe. Leonie opened a paper sack that held two pairs of well-worn jeans and several of her favorite T-shirts. Around the cabin, she would be comfortable. When she went out in public, she'd be Zara.

Swiftly, she tossed off Zara's skintight white leggings and loose, hot-pink blouse and pulled on a pair of soft, faded jeans and a sky-blue T-shirt. The only thing she had forgotten was her own well-broken-in running shoes, so she laced up Zara's, a true example of high-tech athleticism. She took the cell phone Zara's employers had provided from her purse and shoved it in her pocket. Then she whistled softly to the collie and headed for the door, confident that she looked like a cross between her usual self and her sister.

The secure landline Zara kept in the kitchen rang before she could get outside. Muttering, Leonie turned back while the dog stood waiting patiently beside the front door.

"Hello, baby," Zara cooed with her usual insouciant cheer. "How's it going so far?"

"Fine." Leonie figured Zara knew very well how it was going and opted for brevity.

"Don't be huffy. Your country thanks you. I thank you. We both kiss your feet."

"Um-hum." Zara wanted something. That much was obvious. "These clodhopper running shoes of yours won't make all that foot-kissing very easy."

"I forgot to mention something earlier," Zara went on, ignoring Leonie's response. "There's a man who stays in the cabin on the other side of the woods behind mine."

"Oh, yes?" Leonie picked up on the uncertainty in Zara's voice immediately. Zara never sounded uncertain.

"Well, he doesn't stay there all the time, but he's there a lot of weekends. His brother owns the cabin."

"That's nice." It also wasn't like Zara to beat around the bush.

"His name is Adam. Adam Silverthorne."

Leonie maintained a wondering silence. Was she supposed to faint upon hearing his name? Zara sounded as if that was exactly what she expected. Leonie had never heard her sister's voice take on that particular soft, feminine quality before.

"He lives in Dallas, so you probably won't run into him, but if you do . . ." Zara trailed off.

"Am I supposed to seduce him for the good of my country? Maybe I should impress him with that silver hankie you call a party dress."

"I'll have to slap you silly," Zara said, laughing. "Seriously, Leonie, you'd better consider Adam off-limits. He used to work for my branch, and he might—" She broke off. "I mean, he might realize you aren't me."

"Oh, yes?" Leonie decided to have some fun. "This sounds interesting. Maybe I

should—"

"Don't you dare," Zara interrupted, laughing again. "So far, Adam has resisted all my blatant hints, but I'm hoping to remedy the situation soon."

"What kind of blatant hints are we talking about? Maybe I can learn something."

Zara didn't answer. Her voice retreated as she spoke to someone in the room with her, then it returned to full volume. "If you should, by some chance, run into Adam, maybe you could give him a mysterious wink and disappear. That might give him something to think about."

"He must be something if you're so interested in him," Leonie said. "Okay, mysterious wink and vanish. Got it. Anything else?"

"Charles said you've got a dog with you," Zara said. "I thought your apartment complex didn't allow pets."

"I'm looking for a new place." She hoped she could find an apartment in Houston, or in whatever city she moved to in search of a job, where dogs were welcome. "If anyone asks, I'll say I'm keeping him for my sister in Houston."

"Perfect." Zara sounded relieved. "Gotta go, honey. Enjoy yourself. And don't worry about Adam. This isn't one of his usual times to visit. Bye, sweetie."

"How do you like that?" Leonie asked the collie after hanging up the phone. "Zara's fallen for probably the only man in the entire universe who isn't falling for her."

The dog moved his ragged plume of a tail slightly.

"Usually, men take one look at Zara and fall over their own feet trying to get a date. I wonder what's wrong with this Adam Silverthorne?"

The collie, having never met either Zara or Adam, had no opinion to offer.

"You'll probably fall for her, too," Leonie grumbled. "She's an even bigger sucker for good-looking dogs than I am." She opened the door and followed him outside. "That's a compliment, in case you didn't notice."

Leonie walked toward the lake with her dog beside her, thinking hard. Assuming Adam Silverthorne visited the area while she was there, Leonie decided she better leave him off her list of men suitable for a fling.

Unless, of course, Zara would appreciate having Leonie do the hard work of attracting him. Leonie grinned at the thought, knowing full well that if Adam Silverthorne ignored Zara, he certainly wasn't going to give her younger sister a second glance.

Butch clearly found the forest-surrounded lake fascinating, but he was a well-mannered dog and remained close to Leonie's side in spite of the peculiar way she chuckled to herself.

Zara's lakeside cabin fronted Lake Ouachita in the Ozark Mountains of Arkansas, near Hot Springs. Why Arkansas, Leonie didn't know. She'd have thought her sister would prefer a cabin in Aspen or beside Lake Tahoe where there were lots of men and activities. But Zara claimed to love her Arkansas hideaway, even though she rarely spent any time there. Recently, Leonie had begun to suspect the cabin had been bought for some other purpose, probably something to do with Zara's job. Or maybe even to chase this Adam Silverthorne, she thought, grinning to herself.

Leonie walked to the shore of the lake and peered out over the shining waters. Lake Ouachita sat amid rolling Ozark foothills covered with trees and studded with quartz deposits that contained big crystals. Perhaps she'd go on a hike in search of quartz crystals, but not in these shoes.

She walked out on the narrow, wooden pier that extended about twenty feet into the lake and bent to test the water with one hand. It felt warm, just right in fact. She would take a swim later so she could stay in shape.

Butch showed no interest in the water or the pier. He remained firmly on shore, watching her anxiously.

"You aren't scared of water, are you?" she asked.

He ignored the gently lapping water and stayed at the end of the pier despite her coaxing.

She ambled back to shore, stroked the dog's head, and turned toward the forested area that lay behind Zara's cabin. "I don't blame you. After all, you aren't a Labrador retriever."

The woods were green, cool, and full of interesting, well-marked trails. The middle trail, according to Zara, led through the woods to a set of cabins that fronted another cove of the big lake, one of which belonged to Adam Silverthorne's family. She might as well familiarize herself with one of the other trails. Then she and Butch could head back to the cabin for a well-deserved lunch and afternoon nap.

The United States Government was paying the rent on her Houston apartment for the next two months. That would help, but Leonie knew she needed to be searching for a job. School would start again in two months, and all the available openings for high school P.E. teachers would be filled by the time she started looking.

That would be just her luck. Perhaps she should demand that the government guarantee her a good job the next time she filled in for Zara.

"You'd better gain all the weight you can, boy," she said. "If I don't get a job lined up, we may both find ourselves on weight-loss diets we don't need."

With all the free time available, maybe she could take a crafts class. She brightened. As soon as she got back to the cabin, she would investigate. Perhaps she could learn a craft and become a flea market entrepreneur if she failed to find a teaching job.

What could it hurt to try?

• • •

Adam Silverthorne congratulated himself as he stepped out of his brother's lakeside cabin and headed for the woods. He had finally chosen a time to visit when Zara Daniel wasn't lying in wait in the next cabin over. If she'd been there, she'd be knocking on his door right now, asking if he wanted to have lunch with her.

Zara was beautiful, but Adam knew her type all too well. Once he let her talk him into taking her out, he was liable to find himself engaged to marry her. That was the level of determination he sensed in the stunning Zara Daniel.

Adam had worked for the government once himself, and he'd known the moment he met her several years back exactly what Zara did for a living. She had sought him out at a party in Dallas, and he had realized at once that she had researched him thoroughly. Her well-constructed biography about being a secretary who worked for a special interest group in Washington, D.C. notwithstanding, Adam knew that although she might spend a lot of time at a computer, she didn't spend it typing other people's letters.

No, Zara Daniel was an agent, a damned good one. Just from watching her move, he knew she'd had extensive self-defense training and worked out every day. Her pose as a brazen bimbo was so perfect, Adam was unsure how much was pose and how much was Zara's own outgoing personality.

What Adam couldn't understand was why she had set her sights on him. In fact, he strongly suspected she had bought that cabin behind his brother's property because she wanted to pursue him. From a few hints she had dropped, he figured she had been assigned to lure him back into government work.

Adam smiled grimly. If that was the case, she could resign herself to a long, drawn-out siege and ultimate failure. He felt certain Zara wasn't much acquainted with either.

He strode briskly down the forest trail behind the cabin, enjoying the cool shadows and desultory bird song that surrounded him. The Arkansas forest held a charm that never failed to soothe him, even when Zara Daniel lurked in her nearby cabin, ready to pounce. Smiling with satisfaction that he'd finally be able to get some work done, he turned a corner on the narrow trail and came face to face with his current nightmare.

"Oh." Zara took a step back, clearly startled.

"Miss Daniel. Why am I not surprised?"

Although he smiled, Adam knew his voice betrayed overtones of annoyance his mother would condemn if she could hear him. She was a stickler for gentlemanly behavior, no matter what the provocation.

"Wh—?"

Zara shut up abruptly. Adam could have sworn she was about to ask who he was.

Behind her, a long, orange-and-white muzzle with even longer-looking fangs poked forward. A deep, rumbling growl filled the quiet woods.

"Hello, fellow," Adam said. Of all the females in the world likely to adopt an ugly dog, he'd have picked Zara Daniel last. Maybe she wasn't so bad after all. "Are you a new recruit to the K-9 forces?"

"He kills on my signal." Zara backed up a few steps and almost tripped over her own feet. "Steady, Butch."

Adam's eyes narrowed on her. Something seemed different about her.

Maybe it was her voice. Zara's voice was usually crisp and determined, but at the moment, she sounded nervous and uncertain. He studied her, gripped by something he couldn't put his finger on.

Yes, it was Zara Daniel all right. He'd know that long, tall body, silver hair, and those heavily made-up blue eyes anywhere.

Yet, he'd never seen her look quite so—Adam scanned her slim, curvy figure—so *normal* before. Instead of clothing designed to flaunt her well-honed feminine curves, she wore jeans and an old blue T-shirt. She'd still attract any male eye within a hundred yards, but she wasn't going out of her way as she usually did, to make sure of it.

That didn't mean he could afford to relax his rule about letting her intrude on his quiet time. His security consulting business had just landed a contract that meant his hard work over the past few years had paid off, and he had hours of work ahead of him tonight.

"No need to sic Butch on me," he said. "I was heading in the wrong direction anyway. Excuse me, please."

"Sure," she said in a faint voice.

Now he knew something was up. Normally, Zara would have instantly claimed she was going his way. He'd have needed a shoehorn to shift her from his side.

Adam knew better than to test his luck. He swiftly turned on his heels and vanished the way he had come. A little farther down the trail, he turned off and stepped silently behind a thick tangle of wild grape vines.

After waiting a good five minutes, he was even more baffled than ever. No tall, silver-blond bombshell glided down the path in his wake.

Weird, Adam thought. It was almost as if Zara had forgotten who he was. Perhaps that was it. Maybe she had been injured in the line of duty and suffered temporary amnesia.

Adam emerged from hiding and followed the path back to the cabin, thinking intently. Something strange was going on, and for the first time in his short acquaintance with Zara Daniel, he discovered himself interested in finding out more about her.

Considering the way she usually tried to attract his attention and failed, that was probably the ultimate irony.

• • •

Leonie waited until the man disappeared back the way he had come before letting out her breath in an explosive gasp. "Wow. Well, what do you think? This is why I named you Butch, by the way."

Butch, who had no argument with his new name, remained at attention, peering down the forest path.

"That's got to be Adam Silverthorne."

Butch glanced back at her then resumed his guardianship of the path.

"I don't think he'll be coming back this way for a while. We'd better make tracks while we still can."

She could see why Zara fell for the man. He was a good six-feet-three-inches tall, lean and well-muscled, with thick, dark hair and a rugged face highlighted by straight, dark brows and arresting green eyes. Adam Silverthorne wasn't classically handsome, but he was definitely all male, something Zara was bound to appreciate.

In fact, now that Leonie thought about it, Adam's movements were similar to Zara's, as if he'd spent long hours learning stealth and hand-to-hand combat techniques the way she had. That was probably why Zara was so attracted to him. Adam was the male counterpart of herself, a well-honed, covert agent for the United States Government.

Well, Leonie Daniel didn't appreciate covert agents or their crazy schedules, and she knew better than to think she'd like being involved with a man who could be ordered at any moment into a dangerous country to do whatever terrible deed the government deemed necessary. Adam Silverthorne had nothing to fear from her. All she wanted was to get back to her own business.

Leonie burst from the woods and headed for the cabin, chuckling. If she didn't know better, she'd have sworn Adam Silverthorne was scared of Zara. She couldn't blame him. Her sister could be awfully determined, and she nearly always got what she wanted.

Still, Adam didn't impress her as a pushover. If he didn't want Zara, she had no doubt he'd make it known.

Maybe he disliked hurting women.

On top of that, he looked and sounded like a man who appreciated a good dog.

Leonie decided Adam was probably a very nice man, one she'd love to get to know better. But alas, he was like all the other men she met. Once a man belonged to Zara, he was Zara's. He'd never want plain Leonie Daniel, the younger sister who enjoyed her quiet life and ordinary job and disliked the idea of too much excitement and danger.

Besides, Leonie wouldn't dream of going after the only man she'd ever seen Zara really interested in. She focused on that thought and refused to allow herself to daydream of what would happen if a man like Adam ever fell in love with her instead of Zara. It would never happen, so why torture herself?

Leonie let herself into the cabin, relieved that she wasn't followed, and reached for the telephone book. Perhaps she could call around and locate some crafts courses. Anything to create a vacation to remember where she might meet somebody who didn't already know Zara.

• • •

Across the lake, in a small cove created by trees, two men in a bass boat held fishing poles with corks bobbing innocently on the water. The hooks, however, were not baited. The men had no interest in catching any of the perch or bass abounding in Lake Ouachita.

One held a pair of powerful binoculars, while the other manned a small, spotting scope. On the floor in a metal tackle box, powerful communications equipment waited.

"It's her, all right. Zara Daniel," the man with the scope said. "And she's got a dog with her."

"Are you sure it's really her and not a double?"

"It's either her or her twin sister." He patted his scope. "This baby can pick out a dime in a gravel pit."

"She has a sister, all right. A kid sister. But no twin." The second man reached for the metal box. "I'll notify Smith—just in case." He lifted out a tiny cell phone. "This is a helluva job. Not anything like what I signed up for, if you want to know, but a paycheck's a paycheck when the unemployment checks quit coming."

"You got that right." The scope man peered at the cabin. "Ugly dog."

"I'll tell Smith you said so."

Chapter 2

Leonie arose early the next morning and went for an invigorating swim in Lake Ouachita. Butch stood on the shoreline and watched her, as if he was afraid she might swim off and leave him, she realized, touched. She made it a point to call to him every few minutes.

In spite of her coaxing, Butch remained uninterested in joining her in the water. He minced carefully to the edge of the water, sniffed it, then backed off and examined his paws.

Leonie knew that some dogs loved water and some dogs didn't, just as humans had likes and dislikes. Perhaps Butch was vain about his silky coat—or what had been a silky coat—and wanted to preserve his good grooming.

At last she returned to shore, breathing pleasantly fast. The problem with swimming in a lake was that there weren't any markers to show how much distance she'd covered or how fast her crawl stroke had let her cover it. Alternatively, her surroundings were gorgeous, with distant, mist-shrouded mini-mountains and tree-covered, rocky shorelines. The real problem, Leonie figured, was that she was accustomed to marked lanes in swimming pools.

But the worst problem with swimming in a lake, no matter how pristine and beautiful, was that she was alone, except for Butch. It was mighty boring to have only herself for company. If it hadn't been for Butch, she might have been reduced to carrying platters of homemade brownies to neighboring cabins in search of conversation.

A vision of Adam Silverthorne popped up in her mind. Leonie found herself blushing, chiefly because she hadn't packed her own bathing suit, and she should have known she'd need it. All she wore were the two teensy scraps of black cloth Zara called a bikini.

Leonie called it an eyeful—and so would anyone who saw her in it.

Leonie had half a mind to photograph herself in the bikini and send it to her parents on the grounds that Zara needed a good lecture about her clothing. Flashy was one thing, but deliberately provocative was another, and their mother would be happy to point out the difference to Zara.

Of course, Leonie wouldn't actually send a photo, but it was fun to think about. She couldn't help but realize Zara had probably bought the bikini to entice Adam Silverthorne. Too bad Adam wasn't around to appreciate the view.

Blushing again, Leonie admitted that, although she was glad Adam wasn't around to see her in Zara's extremely abbreviated bikini, she would certainly have welcomed his company. In fact, she couldn't wait to get dressed and head into Hot Springs to find the church Zara claimed to attend when she was at the lake. In a church, she could strike up conversations with the other worshipers. She'd be with other people for a while, and that was what counted. Since no one in Hot Springs knew Zara other than by sight, she could behave a little more like herself.

This lakeside vacation business was fine for one night, but any longer than that, and things got lonely for a city girl who had a lot of friends and activities and was used to being surrounded by other human beings.

• • •

Adam Silverthorne stood in the shadows of the trees and watched the silver-haired goddess rise from the water. Zara chased him constantly when she was around, but in spite of that, he couldn't stop staring. No man, he excused himself, could deny she was a stunning woman.

He watched her speak to her dog, the ugliest collie he had ever seen in his life, and scratch behind the animal's ears lovingly. The dog gazed up adoringly at her. Adam couldn't blame him. Then she tossed a towel over her shoulder and walked toward her cabin, one hand resting on the collie's head.

Adam's eyes narrowed. She didn't even walk the way Zara usually did, with that graceful, in-and-out glide common to martial-arts students of many years' standing. She walked the way an ordinary, athletic woman would walk, with grace and control, but the glide was missing.

Something was up with Zara Daniel. The more Adam thought about it, the more curious he grew to find out what was going on. Since he'd completed his work last night, he figured he had a little time before starting on his next project. The question was how could he go about checking Zara out so she wouldn't think he was interested in her?

Lately, Zara had begun attending the same church he did, no doubt as another means of crossing his path as often as possible. He'd even debated attending another church in order to avoid her.

Coming face to face with Zara in church was a lot safer than meeting her on a secluded path in the woods, he decided.

Many people favored casual dress at church during the summer resort season in Hot Springs, but Adam had been reared by strict, old-fashioned parents who believed in wearing one's best clothing. He donned the one suit he'd brought along for his week's stay at the lake and hopped into his open Jeep. If the woman in Zara's cabin was the real Zara Daniel, she would be right behind him.

She was, more or less. About ten minutes after he'd arrived and chosen a seat in the church sanctuary where he'd be screened from general view, Zara came hesitantly down the aisle, glancing up at the stained glass windows as if this was the first time she'd been inside the church.

Adam stared. Never had he seen Zara look so diffident. Not that she appeared that way to most observers, but he was familiar with the brassy, almost comically overdone way she usually flaunted herself and her charms. This woman looked and behaved the way—he frowned, puzzled—a quiet, unassuming woman would. Except for the short white dress she wore that accentuated her long, tanned legs and hugged her shapely bottom, that is. Every male eye in the church watched her appreciatively.

The service hadn't begun yet; people still entered and settled into pews, Curious, Adam waited until she had chosen a seat beside the aisle, then rose and approached her. No doubt he'd be sorry, but he couldn't wait another minute to find out what was going on with Zara. He sincerely hoped she hadn't been injured in the line of duty.

She never noticed him, she was so busy studying the sanctuary and smiling at people. Definitely, something was up. Adam had to lean over her in order to get her attention. When he finally did, she didn't appear particularly thrilled to see him.

"Good morning, Miss Daniel," he said with the formal courtesy he was always careful to use around Zara. "Is this seat taken?"

She blinked at him, clearly startled. "What?"

"This seat." He pointed to the empty spot beside her. "Is it taken?"

"I don't think so." She actually turned to look at the vacant spot on the pew.

She appeared so dumbfounded, Adam almost laughed aloud. Before she could decide the seat was taken, he slid in front of her and sat down beside her. The moment he was ensconced, she stared at him the way she would a water moccasin.

"What's wrong?" he asked, unable to keep from smiling. "Did I forget to wipe off a big spot of shaving soap?"

"Of course not," she said faintly. "I was just—" She stopped and seemed to gather herself. "I mean, I was surprised to see you, that's all."

This version of Zara Daniel didn't know him. That much was clear. He decided to have some real fun, and perhaps find out what was going on at the same time.

"I don't see why," he said. "After all, we're having lunch together. Remember?"

Her eyes went wide, but she recovered quickly. "I'm sorry. I thought that was canceled. My mistake, obviously. Where are we going?"

Adam had to hand it to her. She had neatly turned the tables on him. Now he had committed himself to a lunch date with her, something he'd sworn he'd never be trapped into. He searched his mind quickly for the most crowded and unromantic lunch spot in Hot Springs.

"We're going to the cafeteria with the rest of the after-church crowd, where else?" He smiled with an effort, wondering what this was going to lead to, and reached for a hymnal. "It's about the only place capable of serving dozens of people within fifteen minutes after all the churches let out on Sunday mornings."

"Oh." Zara reached for a hymnal, also. "That sounds wonderful."

She looked so cautious, Adam wondered what she really thought.

"Where's Butch?" he asked.

"Butch is still in the cabin," she said. "He's really insulted about being left behind. Maybe I'd better order something especially for him so I can get back into his good graces."

She looked more natural, suddenly, and Adam knew it was because she considered the dog a familiar subject, one she knew how to discuss.

"What's happened to you?" he asked. "You act as if you don't know who I am. Have you been injured?"

She hesitated over that one, he saw. He could almost follow her thoughts by watching the play of emotion over her lovely, expressive face.

Funny, but he'd never realized her eyes were so deeply blue. Zara had certainly given him the big-eyed gaze often enough that he should know the exact shade of her eyes.

"As a matter of fact," she said carefully, "I did take quite a blow on the head last week. I was riding in a car that got into a dispute with another car over the . . . right of way."

She was lying. He knew that instantly, just as he knew Zara Daniel was so good at her job, any lie she told would have been more believable than the truth.

Adam studied her far more closely than he'd ever studied Zara before. What amused him was the realization that his scrutiny made her uncomfortable. The Zara he knew would have studied him back boldly.

Except for the furious blush and the averted gaze, she looked exactly like Zara, beautifully sculpted bone structure and all. She had the same high cheekbones and arched brows, not to mention the sweetly bowed upper lip and the long, thick lashes. Her jawline, however, wasn't quite as defined as Zara's, and her eyes were a darker blue. Also—he looked closely at her hairline—her tan came from a tanning spray instead of the sun or a tanning salon.

He wondered who she was. Zara's twin sister, he supposed. Nobody in the Hot Springs area knew Zara even had a sister, much less an identical twin.

"I'm sorry to hear you were in an accident," he said. "Did you have to go to the hospital?"

"Luckily, no." She seemed wary of even his most innocent statements. "I just banged my head on the dash, that's all."

"Let's test your memory," he said. "Who am I?"

She gave him a suspicious, sidewise glance from beneath her lashes. "Adam Silverthorne, of course."

Zara would have given him a smart-alecky reply. This woman definitely wasn't Zara Daniel.

"On second thought, you're not Adam after all," she said. "You're that pesky vacuum cleaner salesman I ran off last week. Isn't following a customer into a church considered going too far out of your way to drum up business?"

This sounded more like Zara, but Adam wasn't fooled. "We vacuum cleaner salesmen are like shyster lawyers. We follow potential clients anywhere."

"I was afraid of that." Her face held something akin to relief when the music director opened the service by requesting the congregation to stand and sing Hymn 135. "The service is starting."

Adam located the song in his hymnal and stood. Zara's clone stood beside him, but rather than cozy up to share his hymnal as Zara would have done, she opened her own and took care not to stand too close to him.

He wondered if he had developed bad breath.

Moreover, Zara's look-alike didn't need the hymnal. She knew the song by heart, all four verses, and sang it with unabashed fervor in a sweet, slightly off-key alto.

By the end of the service, Adam was more convinced than ever that the woman beside him was not Zara Daniel, no matter how perfect the resemblance. He had observed Zara in church before, and not only did she constantly troll the pews with her eyes, but she didn't bother to sing any of the hymns, even the well-known ones. Adam suspected that if Zara couldn't excel at something, even singing along in church, she didn't bother to do it at all.

Further, Zara usually gave the sermon only her desultory attention. This woman, on the other hand, appeared interested in what the pastor had to say.

Adam raised his brows. His mother would approve of any woman who sang hymns by heart and paid attention to sermons. That ought to make him really nervous, but he was too interested in the mystery woman to flee the scene now.

After the final hymn was sung and the congregation dispersed to the parking lot, Adam decided to try one more test.

"Do you want to take my car?" she asked, stopping beside Zara's snappy little jade-green Ford Mustang.

Adam studied the fine, sporty vehicle. Zara Daniel did everything she could to attract male attention, and attention in general. Part of the act, he suspected, served as her cover. The rest was natural to Zara's extroverted personality.

"Maybe we'd better take mine," he said. "I'll bring you back here after lunch."

Interestingly, she didn't ask him why they'd better take his car. She simply followed him toward a silver sports utility vehicle.

"Hmm." He pretended to study the parking lot. "I thought I'd parked on the other side of this SUV, but apparently not. You check out that area of the parking lot, and I'll have a look over here."

He sent her in the direction of his Jeep and wasn't surprised when she walked right by it without pausing. "Zara" no longer recognized his Jeep, even though she'd commented on it often enough in the past.

Adam, satisfied that this woman most definitely was not Zara Daniel, or even Zara Daniel with a head injury, hurried toward her. "Here it is," he called. "You walked right past it. Like you always said, it's a forgettable vehicle, so you forgot it."

"Forgettable?" She turned and looked blankly at him.

"Old Jeeps tend to fade from the memory beside the splendor of new SUVs and Mustangs." He swung open the door of the Jeep with a flourish. "Hop in. We'll race the rest of the crowd to the cafeteria."

She smiled at that. Adam found himself ridiculously pleased that she attended church often enough to know about the rivalry among the congregations of large Protestant churches to be the first in line at the cafeterias after Sunday morning services in many Southern cities. His mother would definitely approve.

Adam stopped himself. He was busy building his business. He couldn't afford to get interested in a woman, no matter how fascinating a mystery she presented.

But just this one lunch, he reasoned, wouldn't make much difference in the overall scheme of things. Besides, he had to satisfy his curiosity, or he'd think of nothing but Zara Daniel's imposter until he did. Once he had worked out the matter in his mind, he'd be able to get back to work with a clear conscience and no foolish entanglements.

• • •

Leonie couldn't believe it. How had she wound up sitting beside Adam Silverthorne in an open Jeep, racing down a series of narrow, twisting Hot Springs streets? She wasn't ready for this.

For one thing, he was far too attractive. For another, he was going out of his way to charm her. The whole situation was dangerous to her peace of mind.

More to the point, Zara hadn't filled her in on anything she should know about Adam—things like the make of car he drove and what his brother's name was. She was going to have to wing it. Hopefully, Adam wouldn't notice anything amiss. So far, he seemed convinced she was Zara.

And why shouldn't he be? After all, she looked exactly like Zara, and from the few hints her sister had let fall, she really didn't know Adam particularly well even though she was attracted to him.

Leonie was, too. She admitted that much and felt a strange, frightened thrill race along her nerve endings. She had thought she was through with men, especially men who had already met Zara. Instead, here she sat, indulging herself by spending time with the one man Zara had ever cared about.

She was definitely in trouble.

Leonie rallied herself. Anything Adam said that she knew nothing about, she would blame on her recent "head injury." And after today, she would make it a point not to see Adam Silverthorne again; she didn't care if she had to lock herself inside her own cabin. She could be Zara short-term around people who didn't know her well, but if she was around Adam much longer, she'd probably slip up and say something that would blow Zara's cover. Then she'd be in trouble with both Adam and Zara.

"How long are you staying?" Adam asked, smiling at her.

Leonie's mind bounced from one idea to another. Adam's dark hair blew in his face and ruffled across his forehead in a way that made her fingers itch to stroke it back. She could barely concentrate on his question, she was so entranced by the way his hair blew in the wind.

Absently, she pushed a lock of her own silvery hair out of her face and tucked it behind one ear. "I'm not sure. My boss may call me back to work at any time, but he's out of the country for a month, and everything at the office is on hold until he gets back." She shrugged and added, "It's anybody's guess as to exactly when he'll get back."

Zara had drilled her carefully on her supposed work schedule. She claimed to work for an eccentric boss who was often out of the country on fact-finding missions. Zara thought this explanation covered her strange absences and peculiar vacation schedule to anyone curious enough to ask.

"What does your company do?" Adam asked. "I know you've told me before, but to be perfectly honest, I never quite understood it."

Neither did Leonie. "My boss is the head of a political action committee. That means he's always traveling, meeting with the people who fund us, fact-finding, and so forth. We keep strange hours sometimes, not to mention weird schedules, but it works for us and it's always exciting."

Adam laughed. "So what does your particular political action committee do?"

"We're what's known to the media as a 'special interest group,'" Leonie said, enjoying just looking at him. Thank goodness Zara had drilled her well enough that she felt confident in her explanation, even though it made little sense to her. "Our special interest is fertilizer companies. We hire a full-time lobbyist to present our views to the various lawmakers, and my boss testifies regularly before senate and congressional committees. Our aim is to keep the political climate healthy for the industry we represent."

"Is that right?" Adam laughed again and forked his thick hair out of his eyes while they waited at a red light. "I didn't realize the climate might get unhealthy for the fertilizer industry. What's the problem?"

"Runoff," Leonie said succinctly, and hoped he wouldn't ask for much more information than she was about to give him. "The farmers spread fertilizer over their fields, then it rains, and the fertilizer washes into streams and rivers, then into the ocean. Environmentalists call runoff a pollutant. We proponents of the industry call it an act of God."

"I see." He shot the old Jeep forward the moment the light changed. "What side does Congress lean toward at the moment?"

"Ours, thank goodness." She'd better demand more information when Zara called again. Maybe somebody could fax her some documents. "So far, people seem to realize that farmers need fertilizer if they're to produce bigger and better crops. But the environmentalists are demanding what they call 'sustainable agriculture.'"

"That's a synonym for the farming methods in vogue a hundred years ago, right?"

"Right." Definitely, she needed more information—the sooner, the better. Adam had no right to be so interested or so knowledgeable. "The environmentalists want everyone to switch to organic farming methods, which will destroy several major industries, including ours."

"That's interesting," Adam said. "I never thought about runoff as a pollutant before. I'll have to study up on it."

Leonie gulped. So would she. Of course, neither she nor Zara had foreseen anyone being particularly interested in agricultural runoff as a potential environmental pollutant.

"You'll find it very interesting," she promised. "Oh, look. There's the crafts place. I'm starting a course there tomorrow morning."

Why had she blurted that out? Adam glanced toward the large stone building with what she thought was an inordinate amount of interest. Talk about shooting herself in the foot. But she had to do something to get Adam's mind off her supposed expertise on the fertilizer industry.

"You're into crafts?" He guided the Jeep into a parking lot a little further down the street. "I had no idea. What's your craft?"

"It's one of those silly things people usually never have time for," she said, and wished she'd kept her mouth shut. "They're going to teach us how to paint flowers on rocks. I've always wanted to learn to paint."

"What?" He halted the vehicle and turned to stare at her.

Leonie felt even more foolish. Her only consolation was that this would teach Zara a good lesson about interrupting her sister's life with impunity.

"I'm about to study painting." She proved unable to keep the defensive tone from her voice. "My first endeavor is a one-week class where you learn how to paint flowers on rocks. I'm sure you've seen some of them around. They make really beautiful paper weights. You can also use them as patio or room decor."

"That sounds interesting. I'll have to look into it," he said, grinning again.

He was kidding. No man took up something like rock-painting.

"They offer lots of classes," Leonie said helpfully. "You'd probably find the wooden toy-making class more down your alley."

Adam laughed again, as if he found the whole thing amusing. Which, she reflected, he probably did. How many women did he know who went around taking rock-painting classes?

"I don't think toy-making is quite in my line," he said. "Although it does sound rather soothing."

"Maybe they'll let you sit in on a class."

Adam jumped out and came round to open the door for her, still chuckling. "Are you going to bring Butch?"

His grin was making her nervous, although she didn't know why. Probably, it had something to do with the fact that he was the most attractive man she'd ever met, and she couldn't even be herself.

"As a matter of fact, I am. The classes are very informal, and many of the summer visitors bring their pets. So long as the pet is well behaved . . ." She trailed off, wondering yet again how Butch would behave in a class where other animals might be present, including feisty little attack Chihuahuas. "At any rate, they said I could bring him."

"This," Adam said, still grinning, "I have got to see."

Chapter 3

Adam couldn't recall a lunch date where he'd enjoyed himself more. Watching "Zara" try to field his questions and make small talk was entertaining in itself, but what really added to his enjoyment was seeing the wariness in her eyes every time she looked at him. Why that turned him on, he had no idea, but it did. He couldn't wait to make another date with her.

Perhaps Zara had chased him so relentlessly, he now felt turnabout was fair play. Except that this woman wasn't Zara, he reminded himself. Maybe that was why he found himself so eager to replace the caution in her eyes with interest and passion.

This thought made him go silent right in the middle of his description of an alarm system he'd once installed that went ballistic every time military jets passed overhead.

They had a booth in the crowded, noisy cafeteria, as public a spot as he could manage, and now he wished he'd taken her to a quiet restaurant full of secluded nooks. Perhaps he'd finally gone nuts.

The cafeteria air carried the delicious smells of fried onions and fried fish. In fact, they both had opted for the fried fish, salad, and vegetables. The food was excellent, but the surroundings were way too public for a man longing to concentrate on a woman.

Zara's clone looked at him, concerned. "Is something wrong?"

He stared at her. The air of gentle concern she wore lent a sweetness to her expression he'd never have associated with Zara in a hundred years. It reminded him of something.

"Nothing. Nothing at all." He managed a smile. "I just remembered a paragraph I forgot to add to a report I wrote last night. Back to the alarm. It turned out the problem involved some strangely tuned diodes and transistors. They were receiving the military radio frequencies and retransmitting them as alarm signals."

She chuckled. "I'll bet the local police loved you. In Houston, that sort of thing happens so often, they're always talking about billing people for all the false alarms."

So. She was from Houston, rather than Washington, D.C. His mind, trained to notice details, catalogued this new fact.

"They're thinking about it in Dallas also," he said dryly, giving no sign that he'd noticed her slip. "It's a good thing I don't actually install alarm systems."

"What does security consulting involve?" she asked.

She looked genuinely curious. Adam reflected that if he hadn't suspected before that this woman wasn't Zara Daniel, he would now. Zara had spent half an hour several months back, grilling him about his company. He remembered feeling like a witness facing a laser-eyed prosecuting attorney.

"I analyze the surroundings of the home or office, point out the security problems I find, and give suggestions on how to fix them," he said. "That's why I know a lot about alarm systems."

"I've always thought the best security system was a good dog," she said.

"Hence, Butch? You have a point. Not many home alarm systems can beat a good dog. Where'd you find Butch?"

"He found me a few days ago when I was jogging in the park." She swallowed a bite of the excellent fried fish with enthusiasm. "The vet I took him to said he had lost some weight but was still healthy. Since there were no ads or notices of a lost collie, I kept him."

"He must have been running wild a week or two before you found him." Adam recalled the big chucks of fur missing from Butch's coat. "So he kills on your signal, does he?"

She gave him a defiant look. "Butch is a very well-trained dog."

"He does have a ferocious growl," Adam agreed, grinning. "It was a surprise to me to find out you were such a dedicated dog lover. Do you think he'll allow me to take you out for something to eat tonight?"

"What?" She almost choked on a forkful of green beans and started coughing. "I'm busy tonight, but thank you anyway."

She looked so shaken, he almost took pity on her and dropped the subject. But not quite. Instead, he did something he'd never been guilty of in his life. He tried to talk her into breaking her other plans.

No matter what he said, she smiled and said she couldn't change her plans. But her smile was both wistful and nervous, a peculiar combination that caused him to think crazy thoughts. He even seriously considered hiding in the forest and seeing for himself what the man who knocked on her door that night was like, assuming her plans included a date.

He was being ridiculous, Adam chided himself after driving "Zara" back to her car. There were better ways to get where he wanted to be that evening.

The sun was setting with a last explosion of golden splendor across the lake and western sky when Adam burst from the trees behind Zara's cabin. He had already walked over once to "check things out." That earlier trip had convinced him she didn't have another date. She had placed a lawn chair on the lakeshore and was sitting there in jeans and a T-shirt, with Butch beside her, watching the sun set.

If she'd had a date, Adam reasoned, she would have been inside the cabin, doing whatever it was that women did to get themselves ready. Therefore, her steadfast claims of "other plans" meant she was suspicious of him and his motives. Again, Adam was amazed at himself for feeling so wondrously bucked up about the realization.

Naturally, once he'd driven "Zara" back to the church, he discovered he couldn't concentrate on his business. So he spent the afternoon making telephone calls and collecting facts. Now that he had them, including a photocopy of Zara's younger sister, Leonie, he had downloaded from the website of a high school in Houston where she had recently taught, he thought he had a line on what was going on.

Leonie didn't look much like Zara, according to the photograph he'd obtained, but he spotted the likeness in their bone structures immediately. He was willing to bet that if Leonie bleached her hair and layered on the makeup, she could pass for Zara's twin. He felt convinced that the woman he'd spent such an agreeable morning with wasn't Zara Daniel at all, but her sister, Leonie.

He paused a moment at the edge of the forest and studied the quiet surroundings. Leonie Daniel lived in Houston and taught high school health and physical education. That was all he'd been able to find out about her on such short notice. He hoped that before the evening was over, he could find out a lot more.

Right now, all he knew was that she interested him in a way no other woman ever had. That ought to make him skittish enough to do a vanishing act. Instead, it made him more determined to find out all he could about her, firsthand.

Leonie and her dog had already gone inside the cabin when he marched to the front door with a covered platter balanced on one hand.

"Who is it?" she called.

From the suspicious tone alone, Adam knew she had planned no date for that night. He heard three deep "woofs" from the other side of the door and waited until Butch quieted before answering.

"It's your neighbor down the lake." He wondered what she'd make of that.

Butch barked sharply.

"I've come to welcome you to the neighborhood," he added helpfully.

He heard sounds, then the door opened two inches and Leonie Daniel's mistrustful blue eyes peered out at him. Two feet below Leonie's face, Butch's long nose tested his scent and found it wanting. The dog's upper lip drew up in a snarl.

Adam thrust forward the covered platter. "Cookies, freshly baked. It's a local tradition." He added, "They go really well with milk or coffee."

The door remained where it was in spite of the enticing scent of freshly baked cinnamon-oatmeal cookies. "I'm busy tonight, Mr. Silverthorne."

Mr. Silverthorne. They'd just see about that.

"You're washing your hair?" he asked in bland tones.

"Playing solitaire, actually," she said, unable to stop a grin. "It's a very demanding activity."

"I see." He pretended to think a moment. "Maybe you could postpone seeing who wins the current hand until tomorrow morning. These cookies are losing their heat. If you don't eat a cinnamon-oatmeal cookie while it's hot out of the oven, it loses a lot of flavor."

He'd been on target when he chose the cinnamon-oatmeal brand of refrigerator cookie dough, Adam decided. Her nose wrinkled a little as she inhaled the delicious scent, and her eyelashes drifted closed.

Butch, however, was not fooled. He knew Adam at once for a rival, and an underhanded one at that. He gave forth a low, rumbling growl that Adam had no trouble interpreting.

"Hush, Butch." Leonie laid a hand on the dog's noble head and opened the door, stepping back in invitation. "He's bearing gifts. Maybe you'll change your mind if he lets you eat one."

Butch didn't think so, judging from his stiff-legged stance beside Leonie. Adam eyed them both appreciatively and resolved to work at winning the dog's affection. It was clear Leonie Daniel was a "love me, love my dog" kind of woman.

"Of course, he'll change his mind," he said. "If he doesn't, I'll personally grill him a steak."

"You're a cook?" Leonie stared at the platter he held balanced on the palm of one hand. "I'm impressed. My last batch of homemade cookies all ran together and burned. I had to cut them apart with a knife then scrape the charcoal off the bottoms."

Adam smiled and said nothing about the two ruined batches of cinnamon-oatmeal cookies in the garbage can outside his back door. "If you made them from scratch, I'm sure they were delicious anyway." He followed her inside.

The cabin was a modern affair with an open design built around the living room and kitchen, which were different areas of the same large room. There were two bedrooms, he noted, and the one Leonie occupied had the door open. The cabin looked like Zara, he decided. Not at all the sort of place that suited Leonie.

Butch, looking disgusted, went back to lie down beside the sofa, where Leonie had been reading a book chosen from the well-stocked bookshelf. He noted the untouched selection of bestsellers and educational coffee-table books and wondered if any of them suited Leonie, or if she had brought her own reading matter. He'd have to find out.

"Let me tell you something, Adam." She led the way to the kitchen, apparently unaware that she'd suddenly switched back into calling him Adam again. "Baking cookies or anything else from scratch is highly overrated. What's wrong with a package of that frozen cookie dough?"

"Not one thing." He maintained his friendly neighbor facade with an effort when she opened the refrigerator and bent to retrieve a quart of milk. Her soft old jeans outlined her figure with faithful precision. "It's the finished product that counts."

"Exactly." She didn't seem to notice his strangled tone. "I, for one, have never succeeded in detecting a cardboard taste in a cake made from a mix." Plunking the carton down on the dinette table, she gave him a defiant glare.

"Neither have I." He had no idea what she had said, or what he was agreeing to. "This is a great kitchen. Wonderful view." He set his platter of cookies on the dinette table before the dangerously tilted tray fell to the floor.

The dinette window looked toward the lake where darkness was settling in. Only three or four fingers of orange remained on the darkening water.

Leonie gave the view a cursory glance while she opened a cabinet door and located a pair of glasses. "It's okay. I like the way the sun looks coming up between skyscrapers, myself."

"You don't really mean that," he observed, remembering her peaceful enjoyment of the sunset a little earlier.

She brought the glasses to the table and regarded him with curiosity. "Why do you say that?"

For once in his life when dealing with a woman, Adam found himself totally at a loss. He covered his temporary amnesia by removing the foil wrap from his tray of cookies and pretending to inhale the fragrance.

"Do I look like a bird watcher or something?" She refused to let him off the hook.

"You look like a woman who appreciates beauty wherever she finds it," he said at last, and was rewarded by her appreciative grin.

"That was fast thinking," she approved. "I'm a city girl at heart, and you know it."

"Do I?"

He knew Leonie Daniel lived and worked in Houston, but he didn't know how she felt about it. Most of his colleagues in Dallas were always bemoaning their city existence and claimed they lived only for retirement when they intended to emigrate to a farm in the country.

"Anybody who's lived in Washington, D.C. and likes it has to be a city girl at heart." Leonie poured two glasses of milk and set one before him. "Sit down and have some cookies. You baked them, so you should get the first one, hot off the tray."

She remembered her story tonight, Adam noted. He slid into the dinette, reached for a cookie and surreptitiously glanced at the bottom to make sure it wasn't burnt.

"You must like something about this area," he said. "Otherwise, you wouldn't have bought this cabin."

"It's an investment." She slid into the seat opposite him and chose a cookie. "Everyone I know invests in vacation property as far away from D.C. as possible."

"In that case, why not buy yourself a condo on Lake Tahoe?" he asked, grinning.

"My parents live in Shreveport," she said with dignity. "They can drive here in half a day."

He had to hand it to Zara's little sister. She had prepared to field anything he threw at her. Either that or she was skilled at making things up as she went along. He suspected the truth was a combination of the two.

"You grew up in Shreveport?" He knew she hadn't.

"I grew up in Crockett, Texas." She chose another cookie. "It's a small town in the East Texas piney woods region—"

"I know where Crockett is," he interrupted, grinning. "I'll bet you were the most popular girl in your high school."

"No, I—" She broke off, overriding herself with, "Well, I was elected head cheerleader and homecoming queen, but you know how that goes in a small town."

So. Leonie Daniel hadn't been nearly as popular in high school as Zara. He wasn't surprised. Zara had impressed him as a woman whom nobody ignored, including her high school class.

He watched, fascinated, as Leonie subjected the cookie platter to deep scrutiny before selecting her third cookie. Obviously,

Leonie watched her calories all the way down. From the few things Zara had said on the subject of food, she considered it some sort of duty to count every calorie and work hard at keeping trim.

It was refreshing, he realized, to be with a woman who enjoyed eating, and who didn't make him feel guilty about every gram of fat he ingested.

"I suppose you left Crockett when you went to college," he said. "Where did you go to school?"

She laughed. "I went to the University of Texas, naturally. Would you like to hear all about my college career?"

He smiled agreeably. Nothing interested him less than hearing all about Zara Daniel's college days. Leonie's days, however, might have held him enthralled, but he figured he had little chance of hearing about them.

For a moment, he toyed with the idea of telling her he knew she wasn't Zara. He discarded the thought because he was having too much fun with the situation as it stood.

"I'd better not ask," he said. "Otherwise, I'd have to retaliate with a year by year account of my own college career. I wouldn't want you to fall face down in these cookies I worked so hard to bake."

She cast a chagrinned glance at the half-eaten cookie in her hand. "I forgot to thank you for these delicious cookies."

"No thanks needed. It's easy enough to see you're getting the proper enjoyment from them."

Leonie nodded with vigor and applied herself once more to the cookie. "Oh, I am. You don't know how good something homemade tastes. I've been so busy lately I haven't done anything in the kitchen beyond open the refrigerator for a glass of milk."

"You're on vacation," Adam reminded her. "However, if you feel like reciprocating, I happen to like pecan cookies."

He wondered if she'd take the hint. An interesting vision of how he'd like to thank her for the pecan cookies arose in his mind.

"I'll have to rest up a while," Leonie said. "Paint a few rocks, swim a few laps, watch a few more sunsets . . ."

"By all means." He couldn't help but laugh, she looked so wary. "I felt the same way, myself. Fortunately, I've been here a few days longer than you have."

She put on a face of supreme understanding. "Believe me, I know exactly what you mean. The lake is so peaceful, it only takes a few days to feel thoroughly rested."

• • •

Leonie couldn't believe she was conducting such a ridiculous conversation in Zara's cabin kitchen with a man like Adam Silverthorne. Worse, she knew Zara probably baked cookies just as she did everything else, with exactitude and perfection.

Leonie, on the other hand, wasn't much of a baker. The oven had to be watched too closely, and cookies burned if you left them in the heat half a second too long. That was why she stocked her refrigerator with grapes and other fruits that needed only washing. Fruit she could handle, even if it needed peeling.

If Adam wanted cookies, he'd get a fruit basket—if she really went so far as to reciprocate, and if he was crazy enough to want her to.

She shot him another suspicious glance from beneath her lashes and prayed to hear from Zara that night. Obviously, Adam and Zara had a lot more going on between them than Zara had seen fit to mention. Either that, or Adam had, for some reason, waited until now to make his move on Zara.

What wonderful timing, Leonie grumbled to herself. She was collecting on something owed to Zara, and Zara was not going to be happy. Leonie couldn't blame her.

But Zara was a fair woman. Surely, she'd realize neither she nor Leonie had any control over when or how Adam chose to exhibit his interest.

Leonie cheered up. Perhaps Zara would be so excited to learn Adam was interested, she'd forgive Leonie for inadvertently receiving his attentions.

"Why are you looking at me like that?" Adam asked.

Leonie flushed. "I'm sorry. I was thinking of something else." She shoved back her chair and almost pushed it over backwards in her haste to rise. "Would you like some more milk?"

"I'm crushed. A beautiful woman looks at me and thinks of something else." He laughed outright. "It's probably my aftershave. I'll have to find another brand."

Leonie turned away so he wouldn't see her face looking like a tomato. "Switch to Old Spice cologne. No woman can resist it." She opened the refrigerator door and leaned inside in hopes the coolness would reduce the glow of her heated cheeks.

"Maybe I'll investigate an expensive designer cologne."

"I don't know, Adam." She turned back with a fresh milk carton in her hand. "You might look awfully funny with all those gorgeous women hanging on your arms." Her gaze fell on Butch, who had come to stand in his dignified way in the kitchen door. "Hello, boy. Have you come to sample the cookies?"

Butch ignored her. His gaze was fixed on the window beyond Adam with such intensity, Leonie frowned and followed his gaze. Her eyes widened and she almost dropped the milk carton.

"There's someone out there," she gasped.

Adam jerked his head around. "I don't see anyone."

Butch growled a deep, rumbling threat and appeared to bristle.

"Out there near the pier." She dropped the carton on the table and rushed to look out the window. "It was a man. I'm sure of it."

Adam's tone was deep and calming. "It probably was a man. People walk along the lakeshore all the time, you know, especially in the evenings."

"It's late," Leonie reminded him. "And he wasn't walking. He was just standing there, looking in at us."

Butch gave a sharp, short bark.

"And Butch doesn't like it," she added. "Maybe I should open the door and let him check it out."

"If it's a dangerous marauder," Adam said gently to let her know he was sure it wasn't, "Butch could get hurt. If it's a neighbor taking his nightly stroll by the lake, you may wind up being sued over dog bites."

"Butch wouldn't bite anybody who didn't deserve it." Leonie promptly decided against letting the dog out. She didn't know what she'd do if poor Butch was hurt by a hostile stranger.

"I'll go out and see who it is," Adam said, sliding out of the dinette. "Pour me another glass of that milk. I'll need it after I finish subduing this prowler."

Leonie made a face at his back. This was just what she needed to make her vacation complete—a peeping Tom at her window and a man who made fun of her concerns.

When Adam reached the door, Butch followed and tried to beat him outside. Adam opened the door a crack and slipped through, shutting the door in the dog's face.

Butch whined and looked back at Leonie.

"Sorry, boy." She stood helplessly at the door, scratching the collie's ears and wishing Adam would come back inside. "He's gone out there to prove we're a bunch of wimps and worrywarts. I say we eat all the cookies and drink all the milk while he's gone. What about it?"

Butch wasn't interested. He continued to stand with his long, white-and-orange nose pressed between the crack in the door and the door frame.

Leonie sighed. "You would turn out to be a dog devoted to duty. And you probably don't like sweets, either. Why is it I'm always surrounded by paragons of virtue?"

Butch whined and pawed at the door, then looked back at her.

"Sorry, boy. Adam's right. It's probably just a neighbor on his nightly stroll, and you'd get us sued if you roughed him up for trespassing."

She wanted to believe it, but the brief glimpse she'd caught left her with a definite impression of someone who was interested in watching the goings-on in her kitchen. The thought made her both angry and scared.

Wait until she heard from Zara. She'd have a few things to say about the so-called "safety" of this job.

The door opened, and Adam had to shove Butch back before he could enter. The dog practically quivered in his eagerness to get outside.

"There's no one out there," Adam reported, in tones that said, "I told you so."

Leonie looked at Butch. "Butch has sharper senses than we do, and he says there was somebody out there."

"Well, he's not out there now." Adam took her arm and gently turned her toward the kitchen.

"No footprints? No dropped cigarette butts?"

"It's a rocky shoreline." He grinned at her. "If you're worried, close the curtains. You'll lose your view of the lake by moonlight, but you won't be plagued by mysterious watchers."

Leonie grumbled, but she knew Adam was right. If she wanted to avoid trouble, she needed to close the curtains.

So much, she decided, for Zara's beautiful view of the lake.

Chapter 4

Leonie went for her usual early morning swim the next morning, thankful she had a large dog present to watch over her. In spite of Adam's assurances the night before, she remained convinced somebody had been spying on her.

Butch sat on shore watching her. With him on guard, Leonie knew she would be alerted if his sharp senses detected someone, so she ought to feel safe. Somehow, she didn't. The sensation that somebody still watched her kept her so distracted, she could hardly swim her usual distance.

While she swam, she peered in all directions, studying the tree-covered shoreline, early morning boaters, and even going so far as to study the sky for blimps, drones, and other silent aircrafts. Not even her own good sense served to convince her she wasn't under surveillance, not when she kept having this primitive urge to whirl around and catch the peeping Tom in the act.

Naturally, no one appeared interested in her. Two big motorboats cruised by, towing water skiers. A bass boat hovered in a cove across the lake, with one man assiduously casting his fly toward the shore, but he was so far away, he couldn't see her without binoculars. The shorelines continued to hide whatever secrets lurked among the thick trees, and Butch remained calm.

Leonie gave up and swam for shore. The only thing she was sure of this morning was that she was making a trip to the nearest department store after her rock-painting class was finished. Wearing Zara's skimpy bikini was enough to give any woman a sensation of being watched.

"Come on, boy," she told Butch with a confidence she was far from feeling. "We're going to learn how to paint flowers. At least no one will be paying any attention to us at the crafts mall."

She'd see to that. She'd wear her own jeans and a T-shirt to the class. After all, she didn't want to get any paint on Zara's beautiful clothing, she told herself virtuously. Her own clothes weren't nearly as attention-getting, but who wanted to attract attention in a crafts class composed mostly of women?

Besides, after starting the morning by feeling like a monkey in a zoo, she didn't want anyone looking at her the rest of the day. It was too bad that even Zara's most casual clothing had been designed to magnetize male eyes.

Butch looked up at her and walked at her side. Leonie hoped he didn't turn out to be a dog who couldn't tolerate other dogs. She felt sure Adam was right. There were bound to be a few attack Yorkies or Chihauhuas in her class this morning.

What she didn't expect was to find Adam in the class.

She signed in at the door of a large, dusty old brick building in mountain-surrounded downtown Hot Springs that housed a crafts mall; she paid her supplies fee to the teacher and looked around the huge, almost empty room. Fans whirled from the high ceiling and windows let in plenty of light. From the looks of the building, Leonie gathered it had once housed a school.

Odors of acrylic paints mixed with chalk dust. Leonie detected the chalk dust and felt right at home. The building smelled exactly the way a classroom should, in her opinion.

Beside her, Butch pressed against her leg and studied the situation. Sure enough, a tiny Yorkshire terrier with a pink bow discovered Butch and growled ferociously from an elderly woman's lap, then let out a series of hoarse yaps.

"I'm so sorry," the woman said. "Hush, Gretchen. The big dog isn't bothering you."

"A good watch dog never rests," Leonie intoned, and stretched out a hand for Gretchen to sniff. "I'd better take Butch to the other side of the room or poor Gretchen won't let you get a bit of painting done."

Leonie drew Butch's leash closer and looked for an empty table. The room was by no means crowded, but single women with dogs already took most of the tables meant for two people. The four large dogs present ignored Butch. Three small dogs took universal exception.

"You're almost late." Adam managed to make himself heard through all the yapping.

Leonie started and looked to her left. He had commandeered a table against the wall. There was a vacant chair at the table, and Adam's arm rested across the back of it. Her heart leaped, then sank. So much for her resolution to avoid him for the next month by taking classes at the crafts mall.

He wore khakis and a white knit shirt that set off his tanned skin, giving him the look of a dedicated sportsman. Since the class was composed of fifteen middle-aged and elderly women, a man like Adam Silverthorne attracted great interest among the budding rock-painters present. Leonie couldn't blame them. Adam was definitely worth a second look.

Leonie pulled Butch aside when a Chihuahua lunged at him from beneath a table. This was no time to quibble about seating arrangements. She hastened toward Adam, towing Butch along behind her. To his credit, Butch ignored the Chihuahua with enormous dignity.

Adam beckoned. "I saved you a seat."

Leonie hoped the joyous flutter of her insides wasn't visible on her face. "Were the woodworking classes filled up?"

"I decided I was destined to be a great painter at birth. Unfortunately, my parents put me in summer sports clubs rather than painting classes, so I never had the chance to realize my full potential."

She couldn't help but laugh as she took the chair he courteously held for her. "Same here. I spent my summers at the swimming pool. My parents were determined that I was going to learn how to swim and how to save lives."

Why had she said that? He was almost certain to invite her to go for a swim with him on the grounds that he needed a certified life-saver in the water with him. Reminding herself that Zara, also, was certified in life-saving, Leonie tried to relax.

That proved impossible. Adam sat so close, the fresh, spicy scent of his aftershave enticed her senses. She even fancied she could feel the heat and strength of his arm where it lay across the back of her chair.

"Well?" Adam said, lifting his dark brows. "Did you have any more incidents last night after I left?"

"Incidents?" She frowned in an effort to concentrate on his words. "You mean did the peeping Tom come back? Not that I know of. I pulled the curtains and went to bed."

"Good for you."

She pretended to busy herself seeing to Butch's comfort so she wouldn't glare at Adam. No doubt, he meant to be complimentary, but she knew very well when a man was making light of her concerns. Adam might be the most impressive man she'd ever met, but he wasn't getting away with that.

"I've said something?" he asked, after an interval.

Leonie glanced his way briefly then transferred her attention pointedly to the art supplies before her. "I hope not. Men who make fun of me get black moustaches painted on their faces."

"You think I'm making fun of you?" He looked chagrinned, to his credit. "Nothing of the sort. But you have to admit, it's a lot more likely that somebody was just walking by on the shore last night and happened to look in your window at the same moment you saw him."

Leonie decided to say nothing of her constant feeling of being under surveillance that morning. After all, that was why she was here, so that unnamed people spying on Zara would have someone to watch. Above all, she could not blow Zara's cover.

She just wished being spied on didn't give her such an uncomfortable feeling.

"You're probably right." She directed his gaze to the art supplies and resolved to say nothing more to Adam about being watched. "Look at this. Black is the only paint available. I thought we were going to paint flowers."

Adam gave the supplies a cursory glance. "The teacher probably doesn't want us to get too carried away by our new abilities."

Leonie smothered laughter. "Maybe you're right. Although I don't know of any flowers that are black."

"There are black roses. A friend sent some to his wife once, for their anniversary."

"Black roses?"

"They were supposed to be red," Adam said, grinning. "Deep red. Unfortunately, the red was so deep, the wife identified them as black and took his romantic gesture another way."

"You have to admit, it doesn't sound good," Leonie said, interested in spite of herself. "What are black roses supposed to mean?"

"According to her, they implied a death curse." Adam was laughing, even as his warm, appreciative green gaze rested on her face. "He spent about three nights at my place, thanks to a flower shop clerk who refused to call his wife and admit that she'd interpreted 'deep red' a little too deeply."

"The wife must have been rather superstitious." Leonie found herself unable to meet Adam's intense gaze for very long. "Who would ever think of something like that?"

"You aren't superstitious?" Adam asked, watching her.

"Who, me?" She suspected Adam was quizzing her to see if she was easily spooked. "I'm always crossing paths with black cats and walking under ladders. So far, so good."

"I'll bet you even open umbrellas in the house."

Leonie faced him. "Is there something wrong with that?"

"Never mind." Adam chuckled, still gazing into her face with an intensity Leonie found uncomfortable. "We'll cross that bridge when we come to it."

"I don't understand."

"I'm not sure I do, either."

Before Leonie could reply, the teacher called for their attention. It was a good thing. Another moment of that intense stare, and she'd have painted that moustache on Adam's face anyway.

She hoped Zara called that evening. Leonie had a few things to say to her about the alleged safety of her current job as a stand-in—and a lot to ask about Zara's relationship with Adam Silverthorne.

• • •

The man in the boat across the lake from Zara Daniel's property relentlessly cast his fly and watched the cabin. Around noon, his partner trolled up in an aluminum bass boat, dragging a full stringer of fish behind him.

The partner, Bolt, halted his motor. Observers would have noticed nothing but two dedicated fishermen, comparing catches.

"We got a problem," Bolt said.

"Says who? The guy didn't spend the night. In fact, he left at ten. Far as I could tell, they sat at the kitchen table eating cookies the entire time."

"Smith says the woman isn't Zara Daniel."

"What the hell does he know?" the fly fisherman, Lloyd, exploded. "I'm the one sitting out here throwing this stupid bug all over the water and hanging around outside her windows, and I say it's Zara Daniel."

"An operative saw Zara Daniel early this morning in Istanbul. He's certain it was her."

"He's wrong," Lloyd stated, and cast his fly again.

"Smith thinks we're wasting the organization's time and money."

"I'll go along with that," Lloyd said in sour tones. "I've been on her two days, and so far the most exciting thing she's done is swim in the lake."

"That was exciting, all right."

For a moment, the two men dwelled on visions of Zara Daniel in her tiny bikini.

"So what are we supposed to do now?" Lloyd asked. "If Smith doesn't think we're keeping Zara Daniel under surveillance, then why are we still here? This was all his idea in the first place."

"I argued with him, said the operative didn't know what he was doing, needed to get his eyes checked, the works," Bolt said. "So Smith's going to take a few days and check it out further. In the meantime, he's hinting that we're incompetent and he might need to replace us. He seems to think we should have noticed the switch."

"He can replace me anytime," Lloyd growled. "I hate lakes and fishing poles."

But both men knew the kind of replacement Smith had in mind had nothing to do with reassigning them to other fields of endeavor.

"Keep watching her," Bolt said. "We're supposed to log her activities and visitors until further notice. And if the woman turns out not to be Zara Daniel—"

He didn't need to finish the sentence. Even new hires like them knew the penalty for failure.

Neither man intended to fail in this simple assignment.

"I'll get some photographs and send them to him. We'll let Smith be the one to tell us this is the wrong woman." Lloyd shrugged. "He sent us here to watch Zara Daniel, and if this isn't

Zara Daniel, then who is she? We're just the peons, and we go where he sends us. It's his job to tell us where the subject is."

Bolt agreed. "Smith can go soak his head. Tell you what. If we get word that this isn't Zara Daniel, we're done."

In more ways than one, they both thought.

• • •

Adam decided, after two hours of instruction in basic rock painting, that he could take it or leave it. Preferably, leave it. What he really wanted to take was Leonie Daniel, and from the prickly expression she'd developed, he had about as much chance of that as he had of selling his current artistic effort for a million dollars.

He wondered what on earth he'd said to offend her.

Leonie had painted a fist-sized, oval rock with a black base coat and was now assiduously practicing drawing primroses on a sheet of paper. Her expression indicated this was the most important job of her life, and she didn't intend to mess it up. Nor did she have time to waste, conversing with a guy named Adam.

Well, he wasn't going to let her get away with that.

"You've made that petal too small." He pointed with his pencil.

"You weren't listening." She lifted her long lashes to give him a chastening stare. "You're supposed to make some of them smaller. *Verisimilitude*."

She was right. He hadn't been listening. He had been watching her. Those lashes, those lips . . . Adam laughed inwardly at himself. Wait until his brother found out he'd developed what amounted to a gigantic crush on a woman.

He had no doubt that's all it was—a huge crush. Puppy love, at the ripe old age of thirty-two. For some reason, Leonie Daniel fascinated him on all levels, and he wouldn't rest until he had her.

After that, who knew? From everything Adam had observed, affairs lasted until the couple involved had worked through the crush and faced reality. Reality happened when the lovers realized they had nothing in common except a physical fascination with each other.

Reality was a real bummer when it came to actual romance that would last a lifetime. Still, for the first time in his life, Adam was willing to take the chance of crashing headlong into reality, if he could have a few weeks of physical fascination—and Leonie Daniel—in his life.

"Veri-what?" he asked, bringing his mind back.

"Verisimilitude," Leonie repeated. She sketched another primrose without looking at him. "Real primroses have some petals smaller than the others, so the artist tries to imitate reality by painting them the way they appear in nature."

"Oh." He glanced at his own empty sheet of paper. "I must be lacking in verisimilitude."

Adam was experienced enough to realize Zara Daniel would have gone to bed with him in an instant, but Leonie was another matter. He didn't want to scare her off.

He'd have to be careful. Zara was thoroughly modern in her approach to sexuality, but Leonie gave the impression of being a little more old-fashioned. He was probably going to have to spend time getting to know her.

Adam looked at his blank sheet of white paper and grinned. He could live with that. Mentally, he rearranged his schedule to allow for another week or two of vacation time.

"What are you grinning about?" Leonie regarded him and his blank sheet of paper suspiciously. "You haven't drawn a single flower."

He pushed his paper toward her. "I was hoping you'd oblige. Primroses are outside my usual repertoire."

"They're outside mine, too." She sounded exasperated. "Why do you think I'm taking this class?"

"Please?" He put on what he hoped was a pleading, little-boy expression.

"Oh, all right." She took his blank sheet grudgingly. "But I'd better not hear one word out of you about small petals."

"Verisimilitude," he murmured, watching her.

She ignored him and bent over the sheet, swiftly sketching in a few primroses. He indulged himself by watching the play of light and shadow off her long lashes and along the planes of her high cheekbones. If he leaned closer, he could inhale the fresh, clean scent of the perfume she favored—a scent totally unlike the heavy perfume Zara usually wore. He took a deep breath and entered something akin to a dream state.

"Quit staring," she commanded. "You're going to make me really mess these up."

"Sorry. I didn't mean to ruin your artistic concentration."

She muttered something about his lack of artistic attitude and bent over the paper once more.

Adam suppressed another smile. There was no sense in really annoying her, but he longed to tease her a little, just to see her flash those blue eyes in his direction.

"What about leaves?" he asked.

She reared up her head. "We haven't gotten to leaves yet. Didn't you pay *any* attention to the teacher?"

"I must have missed it. Business problems," he invented hastily. In another minute, she was going to demand to know why he had signed up for the class if he didn't intend to paint any flowers on rocks. "Something's come up in Dallas. I might have to cut my vacation short and go back to deal with it."

"I'm sorry to hear that." She looked up, concerned, and studied his face. "Is it anything I can help you with?"

He suffered her scrutiny a moment then transferred his gaze to the primroses she was drawing on his behalf. "No one can help me, I'm afraid. It's one of those decisions I was hoping to avoid. Naturally, it's now become pressing."

For a moment, he toyed with the idea of spending a couple of days back in Dallas to get his head on straight again, but he discarded it. Two days in Dallas was plenty of time for some other male to move in on the territory Adam had staked out as his own.

"Well, don't worry about the class." Leonie viewed him with concern. "I'll teach you anything you miss if you need to take off. But if you're going to be gone for longer than a day or two, maybe you ought to speak to the teacher and get a refund. After all, she lives here year round and will be teaching other classes that may be held at a better time for you."

Adam experienced a twinge of annoyance that she didn't sound particularly disturbed at his proposed absence. She ought to at least say she was going to miss him. He scowled at the rock he'd coaxed Leonie into painting black. No way was he clearing out and leaving the field ripe for another competitor.

"Thank you," he said. "But it may not come to that. A few hours on the telephone this afternoon might take care of it." He switched to the subject that most interested him. "What are you doing later?"

She looked startled. "I have some shopping to do—"

"Good. Then you'll be free this evening." He hoped she couldn't detect how much he longed to kiss her. "What do you say we watch the sun set together?"

"I don't—"

She intended to refuse. Adam rushed into speech, determined to prevent that.

"There's a place I know at the top of a mountain," he said persuasively. "It's actually a roadside park, but the view to the west is spectacular. You'll enjoy it." He gave her an innocent smile. "Artistic inspiration. If we're going to be painting, we'll need all the inspiration we can get."

"But Butch—"

"Butch is invited, too. He's obviously a sophisticated dog. No doubt, he'll appreciate a beautiful sunset."

Leonie shut her mouth and looked away. "You're right. Maybe I should bring my camera."

He was going to do this right. He would wait to kiss her until she trusted him. The effort might kill him, but Adam knew the payoff would be worth it.

"In that case, I'll come by for you at five," he said. "It'll give us time to find exactly the right spot and get settled."

When she nodded, Adam held back his sigh of relief and tried to look as if her agreement to spend some time with him wasn't that big a deal. Since when had a woman's acceptance become so important to him, it actually eased a pain deep inside?

Something weird was going on, and Adam wasn't sure he wanted to know what it was.

He leaned in closer to watch her draw more primroses. Once again, her soft scent wreaked havoc on his senses, both intriguing him and enticing him. The sensation brought both pleasure and pain, to a degree Adam had never before experienced.

A wise man would head back to Dallas before he got in any deeper. Since he knew he had no intention of leaving, short of being dragged away, Adam could only presume he'd lost his mind.

No pain, no gain, he told himself firmly, and leaned in a little closer.

Chapter 5

"Are you sure it was Adam Silverthorne who brought you a plate of cookies?" Zara asked, when she telephoned from her undisclosed location early that afternoon.

Zara sounded both totally astonished and extremely peeved, Leonie thought. Leonie couldn't blame her. After a year or more of being ignored by Adam, all of a sudden he deigned to notice her, and the "her" he noticed wasn't even Zara.

"Does he have a twin?" Leonie asked.

Zara didn't bother to answer.

"Maybe he sent his twin to the lake for the same reason you sent me," Leonie suggested helpfully. "Maybe he wants the people watching him to have someone to watch."

"That doesn't make a bit of sense," Zara complained. "Who'd be watching Adam? He's a civilian now."

"How should I know? He does drive an old, open-air Jeep, doesn't he?" Leonie asked. "He claims he's Adam Silverthorne, at any rate. Maybe he's just trying to be neighborly."

"Neighborly, my foot," Zara muttered. "What a time to end up in—Never mind. Just don't do anything to scare him off."

"Who, me? No way. In fact, I'll make sure I'm wearing your bikini the next time he drops by."

"Rub it in," Zara said, with a distinct whine.

Leonie was glad she had toned down the cookie incident and that she had only mentioned running into Adam at church. Something told her to keep the lunch date quiet, and to forget Adam's presence in her rock-painting class. When Zara returned, Adam could fill her in. Let Zara find out for herself what it was like to have to fish for the details of classroom incidents and shared lunches.

Leonie bit back a grin and hoped it wouldn't come through in her voice. "By the way," she said meekly, "I signed up for a crafts class."

"You what?" Zara shrieked. "Everybody will think I've lost my mind. Do I paste sequins on velvet, or is it something even more hideous?"

"Actually, you paint flowers on grapefruit-sized rocks, so your rock garden looks like a flower garden. It's very interesting, and the finished products are beautiful."

"If you say so." Zara sounded resigned. "Why don't you sign up for belly dancing if you're so interested in taking classes? It'd be a lot more in character."

"There are limits to my character," Leonie said, chuckling. "Seriously, Zara, how do you want me to handle Adam Silverthorne? What if he asks me out or something?"

"Oh, my God." Zara groaned with feeling. "I'm dying out here, and nobody cares."

Leonie didn't ask where "out here" was, although she figured it was most likely some hotspot in the Middle East. Zara had already told her it was classified information.

"Maybe you can get a leave of absence," Leonie said. "You know. A family emergency."

"What emergency?" Zara asked gloomily.

"You've got to rescue me, of course."

"Rescue you? Are you crazy?" Zara laughed. "Anyone who wants to be rescued from Adam Silverthorne needs a psychiatrist, not a rescuer. Seriously, if he asks you out, go. Don't even ask. Just go. We don't want to discourage him."

Leonie considered this. "Are you sure?"

"And don't forget to behave like me. I don't want to come home and find out he's gotten used to you, then he starts wanting to know why I've changed."

Leonie choked with laughter that was tinged with guilt. "That would definitely be a problem."

"Yeah, you're right." Zara joined in her mirth. "I don't know what to tell you, baby. You'll have to go with your instincts on this one. To tell you the truth, this is something I never expected."

"Maybe he's about to go back to Dallas and wanted to make a friendly gesture. Who knows?" Leonie changed the subject. "Have you had any trouble around here with peeping Toms?"

"Peeping Toms?" Zara was silent a moment. "Are you saying you think you're being spied on?"

"That's right."

Zara spoke over her shoulder to someone. "I'll have it checked out. It's possible somebody's curious about my whereabouts. This is wonderful."

Wonderful? "You've just made my day," Leonie said grumpily.

"Don't worry about anything." Zara laughed. "I'll be out of pocket for about a week, so don't worry if you don't hear from me, okay? You're doing a great job, honey."

"Hah." Leonie rubbed her forehead. "Be careful, you hear? If somebody's watching me because they think I'm you, it can't be good."

Great, Leonie thought, hanging up the phone. Zara thought the fact that somebody was spying on her was a happy circumstance. What was the world coming to?

"Guess I'd better keep my mouth shut when Adam's around," she told Butch. "If Zara thinks someone may be spying on us, then we're vindicated."

Butch gazed at her from the rug before the huge, stone fireplace. Even though the weather was far too warm for a fire, Butch always seemed to enjoy a warm hearth.

"Too bad we can't talk to Adam about it," she added. "Why is it that men always think women are being hysterical when something like this happens?"

Butch had no reply, but his intelligent gaze soothed Leonie's huffy spirit.

"It's an insult to working dogs everywhere. You do your job, and the resident security expert says you're ascribing evil motives to innocent passers-by."

Butch's ears pricked up.

"That's right, boy. We can't let him get away with that. You'll have to nip him on the leg as a warning."

Whether or not Butch found the prospect of tasting Adam's leg enticing, Leonie feared she found the knowledge of an evening in his company all too enticing. If she had any sense, she'd develop a headache and stay home.

"My mother didn't raise me to stand men up," she told Butch virtuously, peering out at the lake, where the afternoon sun reflected off the water in sheets of silver. "I'm going, and that's that."

She decided to make peace with her scruples by wearing something of Zara's, namely, her sister's most conservative outfit. But the raspberry-red silk camisole-style blouse combined with a pair of white cotton slacks were pure Zara and set off every feminine curve. Leonie took one look at herself in the mirror and ruined the effect by tossing a silver windbreaker over the blouse. Riding in an open vehicle like Adam's Jeep called for a jacket of some kind, she assured herself.

When Adam arrived a few minutes before five, she made sure he found her waiting, binoculars in one hand, and Butch's leash in the other. His gaze ran over her swiftly, with just enough admiration to warm Leonie's heart, but not so much that she determined to hide inside the windbreaker the rest of the evening.

"I hope Butch won't jump out when we get on the road." Adam held the door open for Leonie and took the dog's leash from her. He wore a green polo shirt with his usual khakis and looked spectacular to her, entirely too male for any woman's peace of mind. "He doesn't usually ride with his head out the window, does he?"

"Butch is a perfect gentleman." Adam's warm hand beneath her elbow set off a quiver of excitement in her middle. "How far away is this mountain you're talking about?"

"It's a little more than an hour's drive."

From the charming smile he gave her, Leonie figured the drive was almost a good two hours, and he didn't want to say so. That fit with the information she'd obtained from Zara's weather radio, which said sunset that night was a little after eight-thirty.

She might as well enjoy herself, considering Adam had more or less tricked her into what amounted to a full-fledged date. But she tried hard not to dwell on the fact that she was looking forward to every minute she could spend in his company a lot more than she should.

"We must be heading north, further into the mountains." Her voice quivered a little because she sensed the strength and warmth of his body as he stood beside her, waiting to help her climb up into his Jeep.

"That's right. It'll be well worth the drive," he promised, still wearing his engaging smile. "You'll see."

"I'm looking forward to it." She could also smell the enticing scent of his aftershave when he boosted her onto the high seat.

She was looking forward to this way too much, and it was too late to back out now. She was already in the car, buckled into her seat, with Butch in the back behind her. Ready or not, she was about to spend at least four hours, and maybe even more, in Adam Silverthorne's company.

"What are you grinning about?" Adam climbed in beside her.

"I'm hoping to see an . . . uh . . . a sky blue warbler." She indicated the binoculars and wondered if Adam knew anything about warblers, say, enough to know she had just made up a new warbler that never would be found in any bird book "I understand the Ouachita Mountains are the best place to see them."

"Then let's hope we see one." He headed the vehicle down the long, winding road that fed into the highway. "I didn't know you were a bird watcher."

She almost slipped and said she wasn't. "I've always been fond of watching the birds at my mother's feeders. This is supposed to be the next step up." She indicated the binoculars.

"You need a bird book to go with those. I'll get you one."

Great. Just what she needed. Leonie loved the outdoors when it came to jogging trails and hiking, but she drew the line at identifying fauna while she exercised.

"Do you watch birds?" she asked.

"I've been known to scatter bread crumbs on occasion," he said.

A kindred spirit. Leonie cast a broad smile at him. Zara knew birds, just as she knew a dozen other subjects well enough to come off as an expert if necessary. Bird watching, Zara said, served as a cover for all sorts of covert activities.

"What about plants?" she asked.

Zara could also identify every plant, tree, shrub, and grass, and describe their parts. While Leonie enjoyed flowers and greenery as much as anyone, her enjoyment cratered if she had to memorize facts.

"I understand plants very well," Adam said, grinning back at her. "My job usually involves planning security at plants. I'm especially knowledgeable about the workings of oil refineries and electric utility plants."

She broke into laughter. While she intended to continue pretending she had an interest in both birds and trees, Leonie recognized Adam as an even closer kindred spirit than she'd thought possible. They both enjoyed nature a lot more if they knew less about how it operated.

Those thoughts could be dangerous to her peace of mind. Leonie shoved them aside and tried to concentrate on the view.

That, too, was a mistake.

Mountains were spectacular and lovely when a woman studied them from a distance, but she could do without actually riding a narrow highway up the side of one. To her right, sheer rock rose straight up. To her left—and far, far too close for Leonie's comfort—an equally sheer drop gave anyone interested a spectacular view of the pine-forested valley below.

She sucked in her breath and squeezed her eyes shut. "Isn't there another way we can get there?"

"What do you mean?" He glanced at her.

Leonie's eyes popped open in time to see his attention focused on her, and not on the road where it belonged. "Look out."

Adam jerked the wheel and almost fish-tailed the Jeep. "Look out for what? You're going to get us killed if you keep yelling like that."

"I'm not yelling. I'm merely requesting you to keep your eyes on the road." It was hard to sound dignified when her heart pounded and she hyperventilated. "In case you haven't noticed, that's a sheer cliff over there."

"So it is." Adam looked to the side, much to her horror. "It gets even steeper a few miles ahead."

"Steeper?" She was doomed. She might never get out of this one alive.

"Are you afraid of heights?" He returned his attention to her. "I'm sorry. You've always impressed me as something of a daredevil. I had no idea heights bothered you."

The concern in his voice ought to have warmed her heart, but Leonie would have preferred he concentrate on the road. "Not at all. It's just that I'm not used to mountains. The terrain around Houston is flat, flat, flat. I'm more used to a truly horizontal horizon."

"I think I remember reading somewhere that Houston lies on a coastal plain," he agreed. "But there are some spectacular rises on the freeways. I've seen them."

Leonie winced and hoped Adam didn't place any importance on her mention of the Houston terrain. She comforted herself with the thought that Zara couldn't possibly expect her to remember her story when facing death via sheer drops off the highway.

"This isn't funny." She gripped the seat with both hands. "Any little twitch on your part, and off the cliff we go. I'd appreciate it if you'd keep your eyes on the road."

"If I keep my eyes on the road, how can I appreciate this beautiful scenery?" he asked in reasonable tones. "See that cabin over there?"

Leonie looked and felt her heart stop. "That does it. Let me out of here."

Adam laughed. "Calm down, angel. I've been driving these mountain roads for years. Besides, I'm on the inside lane, in case you haven't noticed."

At these sinister words, Leonie's heart, which had been totally still, leaped into her throat with one giant throb. "You mean—?"

"That's right. On the trip back, we'll have the outside lane, and it'll be dark."

Leonie sat very still and thought of all the ways she could kill Adam Silverthorne. Then she recalled that she didn't need to kill him. The road would do it for her.

On that note, she decided that if she was fated to die, she would die bravely. "In that case, you'd better step on the gas. We don't want to be late for the sunset, do we?"

Adam found that statement hilarious. "We're going to be there in plenty of time. You might even get to see a sky blue warbler or two before they turn in for the night."

Leonie shut up. For all she knew, there really was a sky blue warbler in the birdie books.

She turned to check on Butch, who appeared to view their surroundings with equanimity. He sat in lordly fashion on the narrow back seat without hanging his head out the window, and watched the scenery go by. The fact that his leash was fastened to one of the door handles seemed almost an insult.

The drive through the Ozark Mountains tried Leonie's courage to the utmost, but even she had to admit the scenery was spectacular. Adam kept pointing out items of interest along the way, which told her he was thoroughly familiar with the route. The knowledge soothed her jittery nerves somewhat and calmed her jumping stomach.

He had called her "angel." Her stomach lurched again, but not with fear. She watched the scenery to her right, carefully avoiding the spectacular view to her left, and wondered what he meant.

Probably nothing, she adjured herself, frowning, knowing not to try and make something out of nothing.

"I'm sorry." Adam glanced at her. "I didn't mean to really scare you." The vehicle slowed perceptibly. "Well, maybe I did, but that's no excuse. What is it about feminine fright that makes a man feel so manly?"

He sounded droll and genuinely penitent, and Leonie broke into laughter.

"I didn't know I was exhibiting feminine fright." She caught a movement in the side-view mirror and frowned. "That's weird. There's a car way behind us, and it's trying to match our speed."

"Is it a bronze sedan?"

Leonie felt a chill move over her skin. "As a matter of fact, it is."

Adam said nothing, but from the way he peered into the rearview mirror, Leonie knew he was giving his full attention to the matter. It comforted her so much she knew she'd better find a way to avoid Adam Silverthorne in the near future.

"They seem to have either dropped back, or disappeared," Adam observed at last. "Maybe they turned off on a side road."

"What side road? We're in the mountains, in case you haven't noticed."

"Let's try an experiment," he suggested, narrowing his eyes on the road ahead. "We'll pull over around this bend and see if they pass us."

Leonie held her breath while Adam whipped the Jeep around a sharp bend and pulled off onto what looked like a minuscule shoulder. She twisted in her seat and stared back at the steep cliff that cut off their view of the winding highway they'd just traversed.

Butch looked around, interested. Leonie spoke softly to him, hoping he wouldn't take the opportunity to try and hop over the side of the open vehicle.

"Wait for it," Adam said. "We'll look like we're lost, just in case."

He reached across her, opened the glove compartment, and extracted a map. His thick, dark hair brushed against her arm, he was so close. Worse, she could smell the spicy scent of his aftershave again. Her stomach experienced another of those peculiar falling sensations.

Before she could dwell too much on his proximity, he straightened and opened the map, then spread it across the steering wheel in imitation of a lost tourist.

"Well, what do you know?" he asked softly, pretending to study the map.

The bronze car rounded the bend at a swift pace. Leonie pretended to study the map, also, but in reality, she focused on the two men in the car as it swept by them. Oddly enough, they seemed interested in keeping their heads turned toward the view. Either the view was more spectacular than Leonie had supposed, or the men didn't want their faces seen.

"If I was driving past a car stopped on the side of the road," she observed, "I'd at least check to see if anyone needed help."

Adam grinned at her suspicious tone. "You have to admit, the view is great in that direction. Maybe they're genuinely interested in the scenery."

"Maybe." She said nothing else. In her opinion, the fact that a bronze sedan followed them spoke for itself. "Let's see how long it takes them to find a way to follow us again."

"I'll be surprised if we see them again." Adam put the Jeep into gear once more. "If they really are following us, they'll know better than to let us catch sight of them again."

Leonie stared ahead as far as she could see, but the road twisted and turned so much, the bronze car wasn't visible. "They can't just pull off and wait for us. Not on this road, anyway."

But to her astonishment and unease, that was exactly what the bronze sedan did. Coming around a sharp bend in the narrow, rising highway, she spotted the car pulled off on the side of the road, almost plastered to the steep beds of layered gray shale towering above it. The two men inside appeared to be studying a map.

"How do you like that?" Leonie said, outraged. "They've stolen our move."

"Map reading is a common ploy when you're following somebody," Adam said, mildly suspicious.

She whipped her head around to glare at him then returned to her study of the road behind them. "I don't like the way you said that."

"Sorry, angel." He grinned at her. "I was just making an observation. We did it to them, and now they're doing it to us."

"Did you have to go to some sort of spook school to learn all these high-powered following techniques?"

She knew she sounded grumpy, especially when she recollected that Adam had once worked for the same government agency that employed Zara, but she didn't much care. The evening wasn't panning out the way she had hoped. Worse, she didn't care to think about what she had hoped.

Adam burst into laughter. "As a matter of fact, I did. Map-consulting, bird-watching, arguing, or pecking on the cell phone, surveying, taking measurements—those are all activities surveillance experts claim to engage in when they're caught spying on somebody."

"Oh, yes?" Leonie came to a gentle boil. "And which one of those do you think the guy outside my window last night was engaging in?"

"Surveying, of course." His laughter faded into a chuckle. "If I caught sight of you while I was walking past a window, I'd stop and survey you, too."

"I'm sure you mean that to be flattering, but let me tell you something, Adam Silverthorne. It's scary, and it's infuriating, and I don't like it."

"I'm sorry, angel." He sounded truly repentant. "I'm not making fun of you. It's just that I don't want you to worry."

"You don't want me to worry?" She couldn't believe it. "How can I help it? And I'm not an angel. Anyone can tell you that."

"You could have fooled me." He smiled at her, but his expression was so full of concern and gentleness, she couldn't maintain her anger. "Seriously, you don't have anything to worry about. I intend to keep a very close eye on you."

That, Leonie reflected, was exactly what she was afraid of most.

Chapter 6

Adam glanced at the outwardly serene woman beside him as he drove along a fairly straight stretch of the narrow, winding highway. She appeared to be staring in fascination out her window. Since there was nothing to see outside the passenger window except beds of layered shale interspersed with mudstone and her hands were twisted tightly together in her lap, Adam figured she was actually scared to death.

Grimly, he focused on the road ahead, with occasional swift glances at the rearview mirror. He wasn't sure whom he should be angriest with, himself, or with the two creeps in the sedan. Leonie had been mildly frightened by the steep cliff along one side of the mountain road. If he hadn't been an idiot and tried to impress her with his driving skills, she might have viewed the sedan with more equanimity.

He'd have to check into that car. Although he knew the occupants probably thought they were following Zara rather than her sister, that knowledge didn't make him any happier.

"Are they behind us again?" she asked.

"Not that I can tell." He felt pleased that none of his anger showed in his voice. "I've been keeping an eye on the rearview mirror, but there's been no sign of them for the past ten minutes."

Zara should have known better than to send her sister into a situation that involved any danger. Probably she expected people to simply check on her whereabouts and report that she was vacationing in Arkansas. She hadn't expected anyone to actually follow Leonie's daily activities.

He wondered why anyone would follow Zara Daniel when she was on vacation. The possibilities that occurred to him were not encouraging.

Leonie seemed to relax. "Good. I'd hate to scare off all the warblers by trying to hide in the underbrush."

"We'd have to hide in the underbrush?" He hoped he sounded properly cowed at the thought.

She rewarded him with a grin. "If strange people are following you, it's the only thing to do. You did bring along some mosquito repellant, didn't you?"

Adam chuckled. "Mosquitos won't be a problem at this altitude."

"There is some underbrush where we're going, isn't there?" she asked, in deeply foreboding tones.

"There is, but I wouldn't care to hide in it. Mountain climbing was never one of my passions."

"Oh." She twisted to stare behind her, silvery hair whipping across her face. "Maybe they've given up. I don't see anything."

"Is there any reason you know of why someone would be following you?" he asked casually. Surely Zara had some method of protecting her sister in this event.

"Not that I know of." Leonie seemed positive on that point. "It's not as if I'm doing anything suspicious."

"It's possible they weren't following us at all," Adam suggested. "We may be reading too much into a set of coincidences."

"Maybe." She didn't sound convinced.

"At any rate, where we're going, we'll see them if they really are following us."

Leonie's face, with its fascinating bone structure and deeply blue eyes, turned toward him hopefully. "Are you sure?"

She sounded really worried and more than a little frightened, he realized, chagrinned. Obviously, he hadn't impressed her as a man who would stop at nothing to protect and care for her.

"I'm sure," he said simply.

Such was the conviction in his voice that after watching him steadily a moment, she settled back and looked toward the pine-covered mountains in the distance. Adam felt as if he'd just been awarded an Olympic gold medal.

He kept up his surveillance, but the men in the bronze sedan apparently had thought better of letting themselves be seen again. He wondered what they were up to.

Obviously, Zara was involved in something clandestine and important, or she wouldn't have brought in Leonie to take her place. From his memory of past missions he'd been involved in, Adam figured Zara wanted to lull the other side, whoever they were in this instance, into believing she was vacationing in Arkansas.

He relaxed, considering the matter. Leonie should be safe, so long as she behaved like an ordinary vacationer, viewing mountain sunsets and painting flowers on rocks—and conducting a vacation affair.

In fact, Adam thought, smiling to himself, he was more than pleased to serve his country in this small way. Leonie needed a man in order to have an affair, and he was definitely available and willing to serve.

By the time they arrived at Adam's chosen roadside viewing spot, both he and Leonie had forgotten the sedan. He pulled off the road to a small clearing, where a pair of wooden benches had been placed in a small, park-like area beside the highway that ended in a sharp drop off a sheer, rock cliff. A short, wrought-iron fence warned people back from the edge.

The panoramic view from the mountain cliff took in a valley backed by rows of mountains. The rows went from pine-tree green on the closer rows all the way to hazy gray. The Ouachita Mountains weren't high enough to poke their heads into the clouds at all times. The late evening sun cast an orange glow over the valley, a glow that had begun its nightly retreat toward the west, chased by the dark shadows of the approaching night.

Leonie stared around, entranced. "This is the most beautiful spot I ever saw. When did you discover this?" She leaned forward and slipped out of the silver jacket she wore, laying it across the seat back.

Adam cast a cursory glance at the glowing valley, then looked at Leonie and sucked in his breath. Just the sight of her sleek, bare arms and the curves beneath the silk camisole sent his hormones into a frenzy.

"I found it last year, when I was just driving around looking at the scenery." He watched her shove her tousled silver hair back. The action outlined her slim figure and high, rounded breasts. He could detect every nuance of her body beneath the thin piece of raspberry silk. "We'd better keep Butch from roaming around until he's familiar with the area," he added through rapidly drying lips.

Leonie turned to stroke the dog's noble head. "Butch is very careful. He doesn't rush into anything he doesn't completely understand."

Adam gazed at her and wondered if she had any idea how that silk thing showed off her feminine attributes. Probably not. He'd seen enough of Leonie to realize she normally didn't flaunt all her charms at once the way Zara did. He swallowed hard and forced himself to step down from the Jeep, but he still managed to keep his eyes on her.

Not that she noticed. She gazed at the three-sided, spectacular view of the valley below while she wrapped Butch's leash around her wrist.

"I've never seen anything so beautiful," she breathed.

"Neither have I."

He opened her door, still watching her, and took her arm at the elbow. If his fingers slid up her arm a little too far, she didn't appear to notice. He savored the smooth warmth of her skin and the slight movements of the sleek muscles beneath.

"I'm glad I brought my binoculars. Although I don't think there will be any warblers up here." She glanced up at the three tall pine trees growing along the road that gave the area the look of a roadside park. "Well, I'll be. There's a little bird up there."

Adam reluctantly took his gaze off her and focused on the top branches of the nearest pine tree. "So there is. You'll have to take notes on it so you can identify it later."

Fine time for a bird to show itself, he thought, annoyed. That was what he most disliked about the animal kingdom. It was always inserting itself where it wasn't wanted, from spiders and roaches all the way to ragged collies.

He regarded Butch a moment. The collie returned his look, then bounded lightly down from the vehicle and stood protectively beside Leonie.

Yes, Butch knew him for a rival, Adam thought. But this was a contest with only one possible conclusion, and Adam fully intended to be the victor.

Leonie took a couple of steps forward, still staring upward. "I see some black and white streaks."

"I see pink. Lots of pink," he said.

"Pink?"

He kept his hand beneath her elbow, reluctant to let her go. When she turned to see why he still held her, he closed the gap between them and took her into his arms.

"I've been waiting all day for this," he said, intent upon her lips.

A panicky expression flitted across her face. "Wait—"

He folded her close and kissed her, molding her body against his. Her hands, one clutching the binoculars, came up to push against his chest, but he had no intentions of letting her put space between them. Not when he was soaking up the sleek softness of her well-toned body against his and enjoying every minute of it.

He rubbed his hands up and down the raspberry material that covered her back. If her skin felt any better than the silk, he might just die of pleasure. Heat poured off him, heat that seemed to soak into her cool, soft skin.

The minute she stopped resisting and let him kiss her, he knew it. Instantly, he molded her body to his and deepened the kiss. If he could have absorbed her into himself, he would have done it. The only thing marring his pleasure was the binoculars that kept him from feeling every inch of her against him.

Breathing hard, he came up for air and stared into her face. She looked dazed, as if she wasn't quite sure what was happening.

Adam was only too happy to demonstrate again, for the record. He took the binoculars from her loosened grip and bent to set them on the ground. Then he placed his hands gently along the sharp angle of her face and explored her mouth delicately. As badly as he wanted to crush her against him once more, he knew better. Another kiss like the first and he'd try to seduce her on the front seat of the Jeep.

Or on the park bench placed for sightseers, he thought craftily, edging her toward it.

He spared a thought for Butch. The collie followed along with dignity, even though his mistress's grip on his leash had gone slack. Adam observed that the dog never took his eyes off her and he cautioned himself not to make any moves that would cause Leonie to exhibit distress.

She wobbled suddenly in his hold. He grabbed her upper arms to hold her steady. Butch alerted and studied Adam closely.

"Sorry," she said, breathless and gasping. "I turned my ankle on a rock."

He looked down. When he moved her back, she had set her foot on a large pebble and slipped as she shifted her weight to the other foot. The thin sandals she wore were not meant for walking on rocks.

"No problem." He lifted her off her feet entirely and carried her to the bench.

Butch paced beside her, apparently deciding to hold his temper until he was certain of the necessity.

"I'm not hurt. Put me down, Adam. I can walk." Leonie delivered her protests in short, exclamatory bursts.

Adam laughed. He felt like the king of the world, especially from this vantage point. Both Butch and Leonie looked at him cautiously.

"I know you can walk, but I like carrying you." He set her down on the bench and sat down beside her, tucking her against him.

They both sat in silence a moment. Ordinarily, Adam enjoyed the tranquility of the spot, a deep, echoing silence where the only sound was the breeze singing through the pine needles above their heads, or the whine of an engine when the occasional car, none of them bronze-colored, passed by on the highway. This, however, could only be described as a speaking silence.

He could almost feel her uncertainty and the thoughts swirling through her brain. But he didn't mind the short wait, since he fully intended to kiss her again before she had time to think out excuses.

"Adam—" She refused to look at him, preferring to pretend the view of the setting sun was so awe-inspiring she couldn't take her gaze from it.

He reached to pull her around to fully face him. "Yes, angel?"

Distracted, she blinked and frowned. "Stop calling me angel. It ought to be perfectly obvious to you by now that I'm no angel."

He wasn't about to call her Leonie and give away the fact that he knew she wasn't Zara. He wanted her to trust him enough to tell him herself. He decided to go with the truth, or a piece of it at least.

"Sorry. It's just that you don't seem like a Zara," he said, smiling. "You're something a lot sweeter and more tender."

She flushed. "Well, find something better to call me than angel." She looked adorably grumpy, and unbearably sexy. "And it's not a good idea for us to be kissing like that."

"Like what?" he asked, all innocence.

She fumed visibly. "Like that. Like you just did."

"Like we just did," he corrected, now grinning outright. "Sorry, angel. Maybe I've gotten old and set in my ways, because I've started something I don't intend to stop."

She kept him at arm's length by propping her elbows against her own body, and her hands against him. "Are you talking about kissing me, or about calling me an angel?"

"Both," he said, and used an inside parry from his agent days to sweep her arms from their propped position. "I don't intend to stop kissing you, and I still think you're an angel."

"Adam, stop this." She turned her face aside and huffed out a breath, as if to blow a curtain of silver hair out of her face.

Adam took advantage of her parted lips in the fullest way possible. Before she could react, he clamped her against him and turned her face back to his. Then he was inside her mouth, kissing her so deeply, he felt she had become a part of him.

This time, when she gave in, he discovered he was the one who landed inside a whirlwind.

• • •

Leonie wasn't quite sure how it happened. Nobody had ever kissed her the way Adam was kissing her, as if he couldn't get enough of the way she tasted. Nobody had ever held her the way Adam did, as if he wanted to imprint his body on hers. It was the desperation that must have gotten to her, she decided later.

Whatever the explanation, what happened next was incredible, at least to Leonie. Suddenly, she ceased to be Leonie Daniel, high school basketball coach and physical education teacher, always in control of her mind and her body. She became somebody else, somebody she was unfamiliar with. She simply blanked her mind to her own actions and lived for the moment.

She burned and tingled all over, especially where Adam was touching her. When he stroked his hands down her back, she felt prickles of fire racing in his path. The incredible feelings drove her to wind her arms around his neck in a death grip, and to wrest control of the kiss from him.

Leonie detected his momentary surprise then he let her take over. Her lips ground against his, and she explored his mouth with her tongue the way he had explored hers moments before. Her hands couldn't touch him enough. She used them to examine his chest, his back, and the hard, quivering muscles of his arms and shoulders as he crushed her closer.

Even more fascinating, she heard his breathing accelerate, and felt his heartbeat race. Or was it her own? Leonie didn't know. A few seconds later, she decided it didn't matter. Probably, their heartbeats were synchronized and so was their breathing.

She burned all over with great waves of sensation that demanded more than kisses. When he glided one hand over the silk camisole in exploration of her breasts, she moaned softly and wondered how she could get the blouse out of the way without interfering with his incendiary touch.

A moment later, she realized Adam considered the blouse no problem at all. His big, warm hand slid beneath the fabric and pushed her bra up so he could palm her bare breast. Gasping, she kissed him again, seeking to deepen the kiss even more.

Something tugged at her wrist. Dimly, she tugged back, annoyed at the small distraction.

Butch yelped, a short, sharp bark that indicated approaching danger.

Startled, she opened her eyes. The collie stood at her side, facing the left, where a wall of rock screened the tiny, roadside park from the highway. Leonie looked that way and saw a movement, as if someone had peeked around the rocky cliff then withdrew.

Beside her, Adam glared toward the cliff, with his palm still lying against her bare breast.

"What is it?" she asked, conscious that her voice sounded weak and thready.

"Someone is watching us." He slipped his hand from beneath her blouse, as if it was the sort of thing he did every day, while he continued to study the cliff.

"Who was it?"

She almost moaned a protest when the warmth of his touch withdrew from her starving body. She felt as if someone had dumped a bucket of cold water over her. Her mind refused to work, and her body shivered, where seconds before, she'd burned with an unaccustomed heat.

"I don't know." He rose in one smooth surge without taking his gaze off the highway. "I'll be right back."

Dazed, she watched him stride toward the highway. He intended to walk across the road, where he'd be able to see beyond the cliff, she realized. If anyone was there, Adam would be able to see who it was.

She stared after him. He moved with the same catlike grace Zara developed soon after she went to work for the government. Leonie imagined how he would look without the khakis and green polo shirt he wore. Her mouth went dry.

Butch tugged against his leash, but Leonie wasn't about to let the dog follow Adam onto the highway. "Quiet, boy. Let the professionals handle this kind of work."

She had forgotten that Adam had been a professional. As far as she was concerned, he still was. More to the point, he was the man Zara wanted, and he thought she was Zara.

Another bucket of cold water splashed over her spirit at the thought. But she knew she had to keep reminding herself of that. Adam thought she was Zara. She had to let him keep thinking so.

Maybe she could just enjoy the moment and let Zara deal with the results later.

Over the deep silence and sighing of the pines above her head, she heard a car motor rev up in the distance. Tires squealed and the sound of a car engine faded into the distance.

Leonie got hold of her runaway thoughts. She wasn't the kind of woman who could let herself enjoy the moment, at least not for long. She wanted marriage and the prospect of a lifetime when she gave herself to a man.

Then she remembered her hoped-for vacation fling. The problem with that idea was the fact that a fling, by definition, was short-lived.

This impossible attraction had to stop, and it had to stop now. Today. After today, she was avoiding Adam Silverthorne, she didn't care how many platters of cookies he brought over.

Adam paused, staring down the highway. Then he turned and came back to her, wearing a cold, deadly expression she had never seen before, not even on the day she came upon him in the woods behind her sister's cabin.

She sat up straight, fully in command of herself, and wished she hadn't left her silver jacket in the Jeep. The mood was truly destroyed, and if she had any sense, she wouldn't try and resurrect it. She just hoped her blush had faded enough to avoid his notice.

"Was that a bronze sedan, by any chance?" she asked, when he reached her side.

"As a matter of fact, it was." He sat down beside her, studying her face. Instantly, the cold expression left, and his striking, green gaze burned again with the warmth of his sexual interest in her. "Now, where was I?"

Leonie faced the view with determination and refused to meet that mesmerizing stare. She had better remember that he had once worked for the government also, and he thought she was Zara. If he wanted sex, he would have to wait until Zara came home and took her rightful place in his arms. If only the thought of a vacation fling, of a short-lived romance to remember, didn't tempt her so much.

"You were about to tell me how we're going to find out who's following me," she said. "After that, you're going to develop a plan that'll stop him. Or them. Whichever."

Adam took her hand and stroked his fingers over hers. "Actually, I'd rather kiss you again. That's a lot more productive than trying to catch up to these idiots."

"Idiots?" She stiffened. "What makes you think they're idiots?"

"Peeping around a cliff at a woman who is escorted by a good dog and from a downwind position is idiotic," Adam explained, with an air of exaggerated patience. "If they had any sense, they'd use a telescope or binoculars and stay upwind."

"Is that right?" Leonie nurtured her annoyance carefully.

"And they'd have been a lot more careful not to be seen." He stroked his warm palm across her cheek. "Don't worry, angel. They've probably mistaken us for somebody else."

Leonie melted, but she couldn't let him know that. "Next, you're going to say I'm imagining things again. Right?"

"How can I possibly say that?" Adam wanted to know. "After all, we've been stalked by that stupid car all afternoon."

Chapter 7

Adam couldn't understand it at first. Leonie wouldn't let him so much as put his arm around her after the aborted kiss, and it wasn't because he didn't try. Every time he managed to get close to her, she sprang up in search of the elusive sky blue warbler or put Butch between them.

Well, he'd just see about that. He liked birds and dogs well enough, but there were limits.

After returning her to her cabin without so much as a goodnight kiss to speed him on his way, Adam stood outside her door a moment, thinking the matter over.

She had been hot and full of fire one minute then as cold and sweet as an ice cream cone the next. Adam knew the bronze car had scared her, and she definitely didn't care for being followed. What bothered her now was something different.

Suddenly, he thought he knew what it was. She thought he was kissing Zara instead of Leonie.

Grinning, Adam marched to his vehicle and climbed in. He'd have to do something to show he preferred the younger sister to the older one.

His grin faded the moment he started the engine. How was he going to achieve that without letting Leonie realize he knew she wasn't Zara? The situation added such zest to his pursuit, he found himself reluctant to end it before he had to.

Adam sat in his Jeep, alternately staring out the windshield, then at the cabin. Since the peeping Tom incident, Leonie had pulled the curtains shut, so he couldn't see inside. He imagined her walking around the cabin and checking the window coverings.

He had wanted her to trust him, but now he wondered if he ought to waste any more time waiting for that to happen. He couldn't think up a single thing to say or do that would convince her, other than to tell her straight out that he knew she wasn't Zara.

He found that unacceptable. When, he wondered, had it become so important for Leonie to trust him enough to tell him the truth of her own volition?

Since the moment he'd kissed her and she'd turned into a woman of fire and need in his arms, that was when.

So what was he going to do about it?

For once, the unflappable former Agent Adam Silverthorne had no idea.

• • •

The telephone on Zara's kitchen wall rang.

Leonie debated ignoring the summons. She had no clue what to say to Adam. If she intended to avoid him, now was a good time to start. Yesterday would have been even better. Indecision swirled within her as she studied the caller ID and realized she didn't recognize the number. It wasn't even a local number. She reached out her hand then jerked it back, biting her lip.

Adam shouldn't have this number . . . unless Zara had given it to him. She doubted that because Zara preferred using her cell phone except for calls that needed extra security. That meant the caller ought to be Zara. Leonie didn't want to talk to Zara either.

Adam had brought her home a little over an hour ago, and already she longed to kiss him again, just to renew those delicious feelings. Leonie shivered. Thinking about the feel of Adam's hands on her and the hot, probing kisses they had shared was slowly eroding her decision to avoid him.

Guilt rebuilt her determination, but she was finding it more and more difficult to draw upon guilt when she considered Zara's feelings for Adam.

What about her own feelings, she asked herself. Plus, she had realized the moment she first met Adam in the woods that he had never so much as kissed Zara.

Why now? she asked herself. For whatever reason, Adam had suddenly decided to pursue Zara. What had she done to cause it? Or had Adam just decided he had some free time on his hands, and Zara was available?

This had to stop. She stared at Zara's secure kitchen phone and tried to will the caller into being a wrong number.

She knew it wasn't, not at ten o'clock in the evening. How had she gotten herself into this position? And all within three days of meeting Adam. That really cemented her guilt into something that felt like a lump of lead in her throat.

The phone shrilled again.

If it was Adam, he would probably come knocking on her door if she didn't answer. She grabbed for the receiver.

"Hello." She bit out the word and hoped he'd think he caught her in the shower.

"Hello, angel." Adam ignored her bad temper. "I wanted to make sure you felt safe. Has anybody been spying on you tonight?"

"As a matter of fact, yes," she said. "I kept having the feeling that eyes were looking at me, and sure enough, when I opened the curtain and looked out, there were millions of little eyes, all looking down at me."

"Were you, by any chance, looking toward the lake?" he asked, chuckling. "The frogs—"

"I was looking at the sky," she interrupted. "And I should warn you that any hints on your part of any paranoia on my part will be regarded with extreme hostility."

There was a brief silence, while Adam digested the idea that she might regard the stars in the night sky, or perhaps the fireflies in the trees, as eyes spying on her.

"Why don't you open the door and look outside right now?" he said at last. "Tell me if you see anything or anyone looking at you."

"Adam, I am not going to open that door at this hour. Butch and I are thinking about our beds." Too late, she remembered that mentioning a bed to Adam was probably a bad idea.

"I'm worried about you," Adam said. "I want to know if anything is out there, okay?"

"Oh, all right. But I'll have to put the phone down. Hold on, while I go look."

She wished she had her own cell, but it remained in her Houston apartment. For some reason, Zara had insisted on that, but Leonie had taken the precaution of recording a message about being on vacation and out of cell range before she left. That was not good, because if anyone called her about a job, she couldn't return the call immediately, not to mention the loneliness of being out of touch with her friends.

Since Zara had put out the tale that she was turning off her cell for the duration of her vacation, and no one other than the agency and their parents knew Zara's cabin landline number, Leonie didn't have to worry about fielding Zara's callers.

Since meeting Adam, Leonie hadn't had time to feel lonely, and that wasn't good either.

Moreover, Adam had Zara's landline number. She wondered how he had managed to get it.

Shaking her head, she laid the receiver on the kitchen table and headed across the big living area to the front door. She used the peephole Zara had installed and saw nothing, so she cautiously unlocked the door, peered out and barely bit back a screech.

Adam stood to the side just out of the peephole viewing range, watching her with his cell phone in his hand.

"Well?" he asked, grinning at her. "What do you see?" He came toward her. "A mother ship full of aliens, looking down on you?"

Annoyance overcame the surge of joy she felt at first sight of him. "I see a man getting a door slammed in his face."

He moved so fast, she wasn't quite sure how he covered the distance, even though she never took her eyes off him. The next thing she knew, he had inserted the toe of his shoe in the door. She closed the door on his foot.

"Now, angel, at least you can say you were right. There was someone out here watching you." He never moved, even when she set her heel on his toes.

Butch let out a sharp bark, as if to remind her that Adam had called her angel against her expressed wishes. Leonie hoarded her anger, knowing she was going to need every morsel of backbone to win this small battle.

"Am I going to have to sic my dog on you?" She glared pointedly down at the battered deck shoe poking over her threshold. "Kindly remove your foot so I can close my door. Butch and I want to go to bed."

"Good. So do I. With you." He watched her with intent green eyes, on the lookout for any sign of weakening on her part.

Leonie sucked in her breath. Somehow, she hadn't expected this blatant proposition so soon. In fact, she'd hoped to avoid it by avoiding him.

"It's too soon." She opted for the truth. Even if she hadn't been masquerading as Zara, she still didn't feel comfortable starting an affair with a man she'd known barely three days.

Did she? How long did one need to know a man in order to have a fling?

"We hardly know each other," she added defiantly.

"On the contrary, I knew the day I met you that I wanted you." He clicked off his cell phone and slid it into his trousers pocket. "I'm not going to change my mind."

How had she let this happen? If only she'd already been in bed and had refused to get up and open the door.

She sighed and struggled to think while still holding the door half-shut on his foot. "Adam, it's too soon for us to talk about going to bed together."

"Is it?" He studied her furiously heating face, smiling slightly. "On what particular day this week would you like to resume this discussion?"

"This week?" She blinked. "That's a typical masculine assumption. What's wrong with a month or two?"

She ought not to be weakening so fast, but she was. The problem, she decided, was that he looked altogether too male and too assured of the eventual outcome.

"I thought I was being unusually lenient," he said, grinning. "Besides, we don't have a month. Haven't you heard? Time moves very fast when you're on vacation."

"So it does." She gave him her best glower and wondered if the real problem wasn't her own surprising feminine desires. "That's what I mean. What happened to the days when people got to know each other before they went to bed together?"

"It's probably something to do with the millennium." He shrugged and eased more of his shoe inside the door. "Everything changed with the century."

Memories of Roddy Hillister suddenly filled her mind. She'd thought she knew Roddy well, and look what happened there. Even though they became lovers, he switched his interest to Zara the minute she came to pay Leonie a visit.

It was ironic, Leonie thought with some bitterness. Adam thought he was getting to know the real Zara Daniel, and he wanted to have a tryst with her. Instead, he was stuck with Zara's younger sister. What would he say if he discovered the truth?

Leonie shuddered, imagining the scene. Her only hope was to cut off contact with Adam on some pretext and let Zara take up where she had left off with him.

She just wished Adam would quit looking at her like that. He was really getting to her. Where would her heart be if she let herself believe he cared about *her*, Leonie Daniel?

She drew in her breath on a gasp. Maybe it was already too late. Maybe she didn't even care which of them he wanted, so long as she could have him for a little while.

It couldn't be, she declared inwardly. She couldn't possibly be in love with a man she'd known for such a short time, and under false pretenses to boot.

But what if she were?

• • •

Adam wondered what he'd said. Leonie turned so pale, even her lips lost their natural pink color. He thought back over his words and could find nothing unduly alarming.

Maybe she was a virgin. But surely not even virgins these days regarded a man's natural desire for sex as something so frightening it scared them silly.

He took swift advantage of her sudden stillness and slipped the rest of his body through the crack in the door. Butch, standing alertly behind Leonie, regarded him balefully a moment then went back to his rug before the hearth.

Leonie blinked at him as if wondering belatedly how he'd gotten inside.

"Look at it this way," Adam said. "I'm attracted to you, and I intend to do something about it. If you're not equally attracted to me, then say so now and I'll go away."

He waited a moment, even though he knew he wasn't mistaken in thinking Leonie was attracted to him. When she said nothing, he knew he was on the right track as far as physical attraction went.

"If you don't think we know each other well enough, we can remedy that," he added. "There's no one I'd rather spend more time with than you."

Rather than display a countenance uplifted by this thought, Leonie looked downright horrified. "Actually, I don't have a lot of time—I mean, I've brought some work from the office that I really need to catch up on, and—"

"You aren't going to quit your rock-painting class, are you?" He hoped his reasonable tone masked his feelings. "I'm just now getting the hang of it. We can have lunch together afterwards."

She shut her mouth firmly on what sounded like the beginning of another lame excuse and looked him in the eye. "Are you always this determined to get your own way?"

"Always." He relaxed. "After all, there aren't many things these days that are worth the trouble, so when I find something that is, I go all out to get it."

"That must be true, because I'd have sworn you thought rock painting was definitely not on your list of worthwhile projects." Leonie turned and stalked back to the kitchen to jam the telephone receiver back into its cradle, then folded her arms across her breasts and watched him with a suspicious blue gaze. "How did you manage to get the hang of it when you never even touched your rock?"

"Watching you, angel. Watching you." He couldn't help laughing at her alarmed expression when he took a step toward her. "What's the matter? Am I scaring you?"

"You don't scare me." She moved steadily sideways, away from his gradual approach. "Stop *stalking* me, Adam."

He halted. "Sorry, angel. I just want to kiss you."

The battle raging inside her was clearly visible on her expressive face. Adam wondered if she knew he could read both the desire and the consternation she felt upon hearing that simple declaration. Probably not, or she'd replace her naturalness with the mask Zara usually wore. Zara's emotions never showed unless she wanted them to. That was part of what made her a good agent.

Leonie, on the other hand, had never learned how to mask her emotions. She probably wasn't even sure what she was feeling.

At this realization, Adam's craving for her increased tenfold. He took another half step toward her.

"After all," he added softly, "I didn't get so much as a goodnight kiss earlier."

Leonie gave him another of those suspicious looks that acted like an aphrodisiac on his libido. "I nixed the goodnight kiss because you got way too much kissing on that park bench."

"That wasn't a goodnight kiss," he countered and moved toward her again. "That was a park-bench kiss. There's all the difference in the world."

She watched him warily and even edged a little closer to Butch. That didn't bother Adam. He registered a reminder to pick up some particularly succulent dog snacks the next morning and begin cultivating the collie's friendship. Leonie Daniel was definitely a "love me, love my dog" woman, he reminded himself.

"I don't—" She jolted as if struck by lightning when he reached her and gently cupped her shoulders in his hands. "How do you do that?"

He drew her closer, all too conscious of the wild clamor in his body. "Do what, angel?"

"All of a sudden you're here, and a minute ago, you were there." She gestured toward the center of the living area, distracted, and stared at him. "What are you doing?"

"I'm getting my goodnight kiss," he said.

Adam rubbed his hands over her shoulders, gently massaging away the tension while he studied her face a moment. She exuded supreme mistrust, but whether she mistrusted herself or him, he had no idea.

He was right about her eyes. The blue of her irises was deeper and warmer than Zara's, and her lashes were longer and thicker. He loved the way her brows grew in a feathery arch, and the lovely curve of her upper lip. In fact, there was nothing about her he didn't like, other than this extreme wariness of him and his motives.

Before he kissed her, he cradled her jaw in both his hands and drew one finger gently across her mouth. She parted her lips and sucked in her breath audibly.

That was all the encouragement he needed. Adam wrapped both arms around her hard, and kissed her with all the exuberance he felt inside. An instant later, for the second time in his life, he lost control of everything.

Leonie's arms went around his neck, and he felt her fingernails in his hair. At the same time, she moved so far into his embrace, he could feel the pounding of her heart against his.

The next thing he knew, they were on the sofa together, still kissing madly. He presumed she had maneuvered them there, because he sure couldn't remember doing it.

Her mouth was sweet and wild. She kissed him and let her hands slide over him, as if she had never been so close to a man before and felt driven to explore him.

Adam didn't mind being explored. In fact, he thought it was a shame she might finally learn enough about him and not want to examine him so minutely any more. He could really enjoy serving as a woman's learning experience.

So long as the woman was Leonie Daniel. And so long as she didn't go off and try to learn more with some other man.

"You're mine," he said, when that thought hit.

Her eyes opened slightly and glittered with blue fire. "Yes."

Even his blood sang with victory. He seized control of the moment and turned her so that they lay side by side on the sofa before the fireplace.

On the hearth rug, Butch lifted his noble head and took note of the situation but appeared to realize there was nothing he could do about it. He returned to his nap.

Adam slipped his hands beneath her silk camisole. How it had come untucked from her trousers, he wasn't sure, but he was glad that it had. It saved him the trouble of tugging it free and perhaps calling her attention to what he was doing.

Not that she would have noticed. She was as caught up in the magic they made together as he was. When she felt his hands slide behind her back and unhook her bra, she made no protest. But when he covered her bare breasts with his palms, she jolted as if she'd been zapped by a lightning bolt. Her back arched, pushing her further into his hands, even though her eyes popped open and she gave a startled gasp.

Her reaction drove Adam to use his thumbs to make little circling movements around her nipples while his tongue explored every square centimeter of her mouth.

The soft moans she made sent his senses into orbit. He jerked the camisole up to uncover her breasts. The nipples were erect, and he found the sight so beautiful, he lay staring down at her for long moments. She was lovely, perfect, made just for him. The light blue tracings of the veins in her breasts beneath the translucent, pale skin made her look almost too delicate for the things he wanted to do to her.

When she whimpered, he touched her breast tenderly with his tongue then took her into his mouth, sucking gently. If he managed to last through the next five minutes, it would be a miracle. If he thought he wanted her earlier, he now thought he might die if he didn't have her.

On that thought, he got up from the couch, lifted her in his arms and strode toward the bedroom, still kissing her.

•••

Leonie had no idea how she got from the big living room of the cabin to the bedroom and she didn't much care. What counted was that she lay on the bed with Adam on top of her, touching every inch of her body, and she loved it. She loved the weight of his body and the heat that radiated from him into her that set her on fire.

She forked her fingers through his dark hair and used it to hold his face still so she could explore his face with her lips. When she had finished, he did the same to her, touching her eyelids and her nose and everything in between with his lips and tongue.

While he examined her face with his mouth, his hands slid beneath the raspberry silk blouse she still wore and palmed her breasts. The sensation burned through her entire body, all the way to her core. She had never felt anything like it in her life and she wanted more of it. Much, much more. Her breath left her in a long, keening moan that would have shocked her if she hadn't been so busy experiencing the incredible feelings his thumbs created when they rubbed across her nipples.

She would die if the fires raging through her grew any hotter. Or so she thought, until she felt the cool air on her skin when he pulled her top off over her head and tossed it aside, then covered her breast with his hot mouth. The exquisite drawing sensation was unlike anything she had ever experienced before in her life.

Leonie cried out and arched her back in an effort to get closer to that source of intense pleasure. When his mouth left her to transfer to her other breast, she felt bereft, until the pleasure struck again with even greater intensity.

"Easy, angel," he said, as well as he was able while he worked her slacks off. "Don't worry. I'm not about to stop."

If he wanted her pants off, he should have asked, she thought with what was left of her mind. She lifted her hips and helped him take her panties off along with the slacks then she flung one leg across his to draw him closer.

But now he wore too many clothes, so she attacked his belt and zipper with fingers that fumbled. She gave up the fight and slid her hands beneath his shirt, savoring the heat and hardness of his chest muscles beneath her sensitive fingertips.

"You're going to kill me yet." He wrestled off his trousers and boxer shorts and ripped his polo shirt up over his head then turned back to stare at her. "You're the most beautiful thing I've ever seen in my life."

She sat up and pounced on him and they rolled together to the center of the bed. Leonie ran her hands over him, entranced at his maleness and the feel of the hard muscle and bone beneath her fingers. He returned the favor and appeared equally enchanted by her feminine attributes.

She burned all over and craved more of the fire. She reached up as he hovered above her and pulled him down for a searching, lingering kiss. He obliged and caressed her breasts with his hands in a way that built the fires within her into a conflagration so wild it consumed him as well as her.

"Hold still, angel," he whispered against her hair. "I don't want to hurt you."

She groaned aloud when he entered her body at last, certain she would die if he didn't fill her quickly and deeply. He moved inside her, slowly at first, then with all the passion and fire she wanted, filling her and satisfying her in ways she had never dreamed of.

In fact, the experience satisfied her so much, she screamed with intense pleasure and felt vaguely surprised to recognize her own voice mixing with Adam's groan of satisfaction. In the silent aftermath, she lay in complete relaxation and tried to catch her breath.

Leonie closed her eyes and snuggled her face into his shoulder. Somewhere out there lurked a set of very good reasons why she shouldn't have done this, but at the moment, she didn't regret a thing. How could she, when she knew very well that this pleasure she had just experienced was that once-in-a-lifetime thing, something one was lucky to find wherever one found it.

She had found it with Adam, who thought she was Zara.

Leonie drew in a deep breath and snuggled closer. She would have to tell him the truth, and the sooner the better.

Everything inside her protested that idea. She had a month before Zara returned, and she wanted that month, or however long he stayed around, with Adam.

Common sense told her there was no way Adam would think she was an adequate substitute for her older sister. Whatever Leonie could do, Zara always did better.

On that thought, Leonie resolved to keep her big mouth firmly shut. She wanted that month.

Chapter 8

Adam lay in the darkness and cradled Leonie against his shoulder while she slept. For a few moments, he had almost felt her thoughts as she processed what they had just shared and came to a decision. What the decision was, he had no idea, but he knew she had reached a conclusion because she relaxed and drifted asleep immediately afterward.

Not a woman who relished post coital discussions, he thought, grinning into the darkness. He sensed a movement behind the bedroom door, which he had left open, and glanced toward it. Butch stood in the doorway, silhouetted by the lights in the living room, as if studying the situation and weighing his options.

Adam wondered if the options included sinking his teeth into his rival's posterior. He needed to grill that dog a steak and the sooner the better.

A shrill sound from the kitchen area shattered the quiet. It took him a second to realize it was the kitchen telephone.

Leonie sat up, blinking.

"Let it ring," he said and almost laughed aloud when she looked down at him in shock.

"I can't. It's probably my sister." She rolled out of bed to the opposite side, grabbed a T-shirt from a drawer, and hurried toward the kitchen, throwing the shirt over her head as she went.

Adam appreciated the view until she vanished into the kitchen then grimaced. The caller was probably Zara, who would remind Leonie of everything Adam would rather she didn't dwell on, such as the fact that she was supposed to be acting like Zara.

"Hello?"

Although she kept her voice pitched low, the kitchen was so close he could hear her very well. Adam rose and went to the bedroom door, careful to remain in the dark. If he'd been a suspicious sort, he'd have thought she was talking to another man, judging from the way she turned her back to the bedroom and spoke into the receiver. He remained where he was, employing all his former skills to listen.

"I can't talk right now," Leonie said in a low voice. "Can you call me back tomorrow?"

Tomorrow, his left elbow.

"Just call me back later, okay?" She sounded frustrated and flustered.

Adam wondered what Zara thought of being told to call back.

"I said I can't talk," Leonie insisted. "What? Okay, go ahead. But talk fast. I have company."

Adam tried to decide whether or not he felt offended at being designated as "company." He would have preferred her to say she was entertaining her lover.

"I'll tell you later." Leonie's voice took on the stubborn note he was beginning to recognize. "What was it you needed to tell me?"

Perhaps Zara was going to order Leonie to abandon the cabin and fly immediately to some other location. Well, he'd just see about that. He could book a flight as well as Leonie could.

"Yes, I was followed by a bronze sedan today when I drove into the mountains to watch the sun set. Can you look into it?" She recited the license plate number.

Adam mentally nodded approval. Zara was checking into Leonie's peeping Tom. He'd like to speak to her himself in order to find out what she might have learned.

"What? Oh. Just—someone I met at the lake."

She had her back to him, but Adam knew exactly what Zara had asked and how Leonie felt about evading her sister's questions. He wondered why Leonie didn't go ahead and tell Zara he was there. Zara was bound to be thrilled, he thought cynically. After all, she had more or less let him know she was available and interested. Maybe she'd think Leonie was furthering her cause.

"No, it is not. Why should it be him?"

Adam's eyes widened. Leonie was lying. He knew it, just as he knew Zara had asked her outright if the man with her was Adam.

Leonie didn't want her sister knowing he was with her. Adam supposed he could understand why not, although he had every intention of making sure everyone knew it before too much longer. And "everyone" included, first and foremost, Zara Daniel.

Leonie probably thought she was stealing her sister's boyfriend. Adam noted the look of guilt on her expressive face when she turned, and knew he was right in that surmise.

The next few days, he reflected as he faded back into the darkness of the bedroom, should be really interesting.

• • •

Leonie replaced the telephone receiver, amazed at herself. She had just outright *lied* to her sister when Zara had asked if Adam was her mysterious visitor.

But if a woman intended to enjoy a vacation romance, especially if it was with her sister's crush, the first rule was to keep the matter private. The fewer people who knew about it, the better.

Or so she told herself. After all, what did she know about vacation romances or any other kind of romance?

But, by golly, she now had a prime opportunity to learn, and she fully intended to seize her chance.

She padded back to the bedroom, clad only in the soft cotton T-shirt she had snatched up in passing. She would not have been surprised if Adam had been fully dressed and ready to leave, especially now that he had gotten what he probably came for. In her limited experience, once a man got a woman into bed, he was either ready to move on to the next woman or to get back to his own life until he wanted sex again.

To her joy, Adam awaited her in bed. She walked toward him cautiously and wondered what she should say next.

He stretched out a hand to her. "So was it your sister? I didn't know you had one. How is she doing?"

"Yes, it was her." She sat down on the edge of the bed and wondered what a sophisticated woman might do next. "She's fine, but if I don't answer the phone when I'm supposed to, she calls my parents. Believe me, we don't need them descending on us."

That was so lame, it needed crutches, but Adam appeared to notice nothing amiss. "True. It would ruin the solitude around here. Come back to bed, angel. I missed you."

"I've only been gone about five minutes." She slid in beside him, still wearing the T-shirt, and reflected that Adam must have a lot of experience with the opposite sex. In her opinion, he could not have said anything more romantic.

"It was four minutes and fifty-five seconds too long." He ran his hands up her sides and skimmed the T-shirt off over her head. "You're so beautiful, I could stare at you all night."

She ran her fingers over the muscles of his shoulders. "I'm glad, because I'd like to do the same to you."

"In that case, look all you like, because I'm definitely going to be looking at you," he said in a desire-roughened voice.

Leonie gloried in the way he looked at her in the semi-darkness, as if he couldn't get enough of her. He rubbed his hands over her nude body, creating heat that was not entirely due to friction. She did the same to him. His taut skin felt rough and heated. Better, he showed his pleasure in the way she touched him by closing his eyes and groaning softly. It drove her to find new ways to explore his body, and she loved it when he did the same to her.

They made love a grand total of four times during the night, if she counted the early morning session when they both awakened face to face and took up where they had left off during the hours of darkness. Leonie considered it the most exciting and satisfying night of her existence, and she very much doubted if anything else in her life would ever top it.

She wished she had a book that would list for her the rules of conducting a short-lived romance, but failing the book, she figured the best thing to do was take things light and easy. She would make no demands and enjoy each day as it came. Most of all, she needed to bear in mind the fact that it would end when her so-called vacation ended.

In short, she must not fall in love with Adam Silverthorne, even though she feared she was already most of the way there.

Who was she kidding? She was *there*.

On that note, she waited until Adam was in the shower before she arose and dressed in a pair of her favorite jeans and one of her own T-shirts. She went to the kitchen barefooted, noting her state of relaxed bliss. After their night together, they both needed a good breakfast, and one thing she knew how to do really well was cook breakfast. In Zara's neat kitchen, which someone had thoughtfully stocked for her stay, she could scramble eggs, fry bacon, and toast bread like a master chef.

She let Butch outside for a few moments, then let him back in. "If he's eager to rush back home," she told the dog, "you get to eat his share of the breakfast."

Butch regarded her with serious attention. Perhaps he was planning an attack designed to speed Adam on his way back home to his own cabin, and that was assuming Adam didn't already have an excuse to flee on the tip of his tongue.

"Good morning, angel," Adam said.

She looked up from the frying pan. He stood in the door watching her as if he took enormous pleasure in just looking at her.

She smiled at him. "You're lucky it's morning. The only meal I really know how to cook is breakfast."

"Too busy the rest of the day?" He came to her and slipped his arms around her from behind to nuzzle her neck.

"How did you ever guess?" Goose bumps traveled up and down her arms in the wake of his caress. "But I was taught that if you ate a really good breakfast, it would carry you all day long. My experience is that it's true. So I keep all kinds of fruit and hearty breakfast foods on hand and get up early enough every morning to cook."

Adam pulled his cell phone from his pocket and glanced at the face. "It's only seven o'clock. Since we're both on vacation, I'm gathering you're one of those early risers."

"I suppose I am." She forked bacon onto a plate covered with paper napkins and carefully blotted off the grease. "Once you get into the habit, it's a hard one to break. I've never been able to sleep much beyond eight o'clock in the morning."

She was babbling, and if she didn't get hold of herself, she was likely to start telling him all about her mornings at the schools where she had taught, and why she sometimes had to be there even earlier than regular class times.

Adam appeared to notice nothing unusual about the way she suddenly shut up. "I know what you mean. I'm the same way." He kissed her temple. "What time is our rock-painting class? Do we have time to go for a swim beforehand?"

Leonie reflected that if he knew how his touch confused her, he'd know better than to kiss her before asking a question. After dithering mentally for a moment, she replied, "Yes, I think so. The class is at ten o'clock."

"Good. Do we have orange juice?" When she nodded, he went to the refrigerator. "I'll get it. What about the butter?"

He behaved exactly like her father behaved with her mother, Leonie thought, astonished. He was helping her set the table and put out the items needed for a good breakfast. Of all the things she had expected him to do upon awakening in her bed this morning, helping her get breakfast hadn't even been on the list. She shot him a quick, suspicious glance while he poked around in the refrigerator. What had happened to the male's quick exit before the female even woke up?

So far as she could tell, Adam was in no hurry to leave. While she cooked, he examined the cabinets and the refrigerator for future reference, or so he said. After setting the table and sectioning a grapefruit at her instruction, he devoted himself to eating her version of a hearty breakfast, and talked about taking her to view some of the local sights that afternoon.

"Can you show me one of those crystal shops?" she asked. "Those big quartz crystals I see on display are so beautiful, I'm dying to see them up close."

"What you mean is, you want to buy one," Adam said. "Maybe we ought to go on a big crystal hunt in the mountains so you can pick one up for free."

Leonie tried to keep her enthusiasm from showing. "I'll bet somebody owns all the land and you can't go on it without paying a fee. Unless you know someone?" she added hopefully.

He laughed. "If I don't know anybody, I'll have to ask around. You can bet somebody living on this lake has an interest in a crystal mine somewhere in these mountains. If not, there's always a shop that would love to show you some crystals."

Leonie felt as if the heavens had opened up and showered her with favors. Although she had dreamed of a vacation romance, she hadn't really expected anything like this, where the man stuck around and entertained her.

Adam appeared to thoroughly enjoy the breakfast and complimented her cooking skills. He then slipped Butch a whole slice of bacon. He even helped her wash the dishes and waited while she changed into Zara's tiny bikini. It was ridiculous, but she felt a little shy when she walked out with a big towel draped over her shoulders, even after the night she had just spent with him.

"Now that's a bikini," Adam said, grinning. "Too bad you're not allowed to wear it for anyone but me."

Naturally, he couldn't have said anything more calculated to ease her discomfort. She dropped the towel and let it hang over her arm while they walked the fifty feet to the lakeshore. Butch walked beside Leonie, but she noticed he seemed much less hostile to Adam.

"Are you planning to wear your boxer shorts, or are you skinny-dipping today?" she asked, dropping her towel on the rocky shoreline.

Adam still wore the green polo shirt and khaki pants from the day before. Pausing, he scanned the lake, squinting into the rising sun to do so, and studied the forest behind them.

"I'll wear my boxers. With all the early-morning fishermen out on the lake, I wouldn't want to give anyone too big a thrill."

Something about the way he spoke alerted her. "What's wrong?"

"Nothing, angel." He narrowed his gaze on a distant bass boat that floated in a cove across the lake. "But there are fishermen and women out, and we don't need anyone calling the local cops out because of a naked-man sighting."

Leonie looked around, but the cabins close enough for her to see all looked tightly closed, and the only fishing enthusiasts visible were the man in the boat across the lake and another man in a small motorboat that seemed headed toward the same small cove.

"That must be a good fishing area," she observed. "There've been boats there every day since I've been here."

"You're probably right." Adam quickly shed his trousers and tossed his shirt on the rocks. "Come on, angel. No sense in giving them an eyeful."

"If I can't see them clearly, they can't see me," Leonie said reasonably, but she followed Adam quickly into the cool lake waters.

Now that she thought about it, she had spent the past couple of days feeling spied upon. For all she knew, those boaters had high-powered binoculars lying beside them. She leaned forward into the water and swam beside Adam into the deeper waters farther offshore.

"How far do you usually swim?" He stopped his forward movement, still looking toward the cove where the two fishing boats had come together.

Leonie scowled at the rocky lakeshore where Butch stood waiting with canine patience. "I usually swim ten laps, but out here I can't tell how far that is so I've been swimming to that outcrop and back. It seems to be about the right distance."

"That sounds reasonable. Come on. I'll race you."

As she had suspected, Adam was a strong swimmer. She had been on her college swim team, and stayed in shape with regular swimming, but she had trouble keeping up with him. She loved it. She found their race invigorating and as beneficial as her usual morning jog or laps. Adam challenged her to put forth her best effort, something she had missed since she had gone into coaching and left competition behind.

Fortunately, she managed to remember her role before she came out with the exclamation of praise trembling on her lips when they finished their race. Zara would never praise anyone who beat her in anything, not even a man she wanted.

Not for the first time, she reflected that being Zara could be awfully wearing.

• • •

Back on the rocky shore, Adam pulled his trousers back on and donned his shirt. He kept his head tilted down so that his hair partially screened his eyes and held his gaze on the two boats in the cove across the lake. He couldn't be sure at this distance, but he would not have been surprised if one of those boats, the one in back, served as a platform for a spotting scope.

That would make sense if someone were keeping Zara Daniel under surveillance. He resolved to check into the matter by making a few calls to his former employer. Zara probably expected someone to spy on her as a part of her job, and no doubt knew what to do, but Leonie was another matter. She obviously found it scary.

Adam discovered that he also disliked the idea of anyone watching Leonie. He had to restrain himself from grabbing the big towel she'd brought and wrapping her up in it. Fortunately, she picked up the towel and wrapped it around herself after casting one narrow-eyed glance at the two boats in the faraway cove.

"I'll pick you and Butch up in an hour," he said. "I've got to make a couple of calls and take care of a little business."

Leonie halted at her front door and smiled over her shoulder at him. "Guess I'd better do the same. See you later, Adam."

She wasn't getting away with that. Adam moved in quickly and bent her back over his arm in the theatrical manner of an old-fashioned stage lover.

"Careful, my pretty, or I'll have to stick closer to your side."

With that, he righted her and kissed her thoroughly. Let the watchers across the lake make of that what they would. And let Miss Leonie Daniel take it as a declaration of his intent.

Leonie regarded him with wide, uncertain blue eyes. "I'm supposed to cling to your arm and refuse to let you go back to your own cabin for so much as five minutes?"

He pretended to think. "That might help soothe my ruffled feelings. It's a blow to the masculine ego to be sent on my way with a smile and a wave."

She actually put her fingers to her temples and squeezed her eyes shut. "What happened to the morning-after fast exit and the 'I'll call you later' line?"

"Sorry, sweetheart." He stepped back, laughing. "You're now in my power, and I intend to see to it that you stay there."

• • •

Across the lake, Bolt looked up from the spotting scope and grunted. "Oh, I'd say it's on. He spent the night with her, and now he's kissing the towel off her outside her cabin door."

"It could be a plan on the part of two government agents." Lloyd, who had a pair of strong binoculars lying at his feet, glanced at the distant couple. All he could tell at that distance with his normal vision was that they stood outside the cabin door. "But I think you're right. Whether it's a plan or not, they're still getting it on. What man wouldn't take advantage of *that*?"

"That" being Zara Daniel's delectable body, which both men had spent many hours admiring during the past few days.

"Smith still says he doesn't think we're watching Zara Daniel," Bolt offered.

"Then who the hell does he think she is?" Lloyd grabbed his binoculars and peered through them.

"He thinks it's some look-alike agent they've put in place to fool us."

"She looks enough like Daniel to fool me." Lloyd lowered his binoculars when the woman vanished inside her cabin and the man with her took off into the woods at the back of the cabin. "So what are we supposed to do? Stay on the subject, or go to something else?"

"Smith says we should never have wasted our time watching her in the first place. We should have trailed the real Zara Daniel to Istanbul."

"So Smith is going to say we failed our mission, no matter who that woman is?"

"Looks like it."

The two men exchanged portentous glances. They both knew what failure meant, especially in a matter considered so simple as keeping tabs on Zara Daniel. Each reflected, in his own way, that this job opportunity left a lot to be desired.

"You know what?" Lloyd stowed his binoculars at his feet once more and gave his fly rod a twitch. "I think we need to prove we've got the right woman. Or the wrong one, depending. Then we'll know what to do."

"And how do you think we should prove it?" Bolt collapsed his spotting scope and tossed a jacket over it before taking up his own fly rod once more.

"I've been thinking on it, and I've got a plan."

They drew their boats a bit closer together and lowered their voices to discuss the plan. Anyone watching would have thought two friends in separate fishing boats were exchanging fish tales, so assiduously did they work their fly rods while they talked.

"I hate to say this, pal, but I think you're right," Bolt said when the discussion was finished. "Let's do it."

• • •

Adam spent almost half an hour on the telephone, calling his former contacts in the government and the head of his former department. The information he gathered was largely useless, and nobody would tell him what was up with Zara, or why they thought it so necessary to rope in Leonie to act as a decoy.

He did, however, learn that the weather in Washington, D.C. was hot and humid. On that note, he clicked off his phone, annoyed, and reflected that if he gave a government agency, the

IRS for instance, the kind of answers they'd just given him, he would surely be arrested and spend the next twenty years in prison.

That meant that Leonie must be on her own because nobody figured she was in any danger.

Adam didn't know why, but he had a gut feeling that Leonie stood in danger of something, and nobody would tell him anything. That was fine with him. For the next week or more, however long she stayed at the cabin acting as her sister, he was staying with her.

He smiled, remembering the night he had just spent with her.

It was always nice when a man had a good excuse for doing exactly what he wanted to do in the first place.

Chapter 9

Leonie regarded Adam with suspicion as he drove them in his open Jeep to their rock-painting class. He looked relaxed, cheerful, and interested in her company, not at all like a man who had achieved his goal and was ready to move on. She felt sure that meant something, but she had no idea what it could be.

Maybe he was at loose ends and needed something, anything, to fill his time.

She considered that idea a moment while she watched the winding black highway. Maybe he had forgotten he'd told her about the proposals he was completing and the other work he had to catch up on. On the other hand, maybe he had been making it all up in order to keep her from encroaching on his time.

In truth, she had no idea what to think. The whole thing with Adam, in her opinion, ranked as highly suspicious. Compared to Zara, she knew most men would consider her ordinary, maybe even boring, but Adam seemed to find everything she did and said interesting. If that wasn't a suspicious circumstance, what was?

She wasn't even wearing Zara's clothing the way she was supposed to. Instead, she wore her own jeans and one of the two T-shirts she had brought along. Zara's elegant little sandals polished the outfit considerably, but only because she had forgotten to bring a pair of her own running shoes. Zara's high-tech running shoes disturbed her entire sense of equilibrium and were at least one size too big for her.

Butch sat alertly on the back seat and regarded the passing scenery with interest. She wondered what he thought of the situation with Adam. So far as she could tell, Butch still looked upon Adam as an interloper, but being a well-mannered dog, he would not take steps to run Adam off unless Leonie gave the signal.

Leonie sighed and concentrated on a business alongside the highway that bore a sign that read, "Crystal Shack." She needed to keep her mind on the "romance" aspect of her vacation romance. Worrying over why Adam had picked now to make his move on Zara struck her as unproductive. Her job was to enjoy his company, enjoy her vacation, and make memories. She would need some good memories when the month was up and she went back to Houston and got busy hunting for a job and a new apartment.

Thoughts of searching for a job and an apartment at the tag end of the summer season, when all the apartments were rented and the jobs were already filled, depressed her so much; Leonie rubbed her forehead to stave off the impending headache.

"Are you all right, angel?" Adam glanced her way with concern. "Do you have a headache?"

"I'm fine," Leonie said quickly. "We just passed an interesting crystal shop. Maybe we can stop by there when we're through with our rock painting."

"Anything you like." Adam smiled and returned his attention to the road, much to her relief. "Just don't buy anything too big for me to carry to the Jeep."

"I was thinking more on the order of a coffee-table display piece. Nothing too big or fancy."

Many of the crystal clusters she had seen on display in the front yard of the Crystal Shack must have weighed somewhere on the order of fifty to a hundred pounds. Naturally, she coveted a really big cluster, but when one lived in an apartment, one stuck to coffee-table-sized displays.

Adam grinned. "Sure, you were. I saw you studying those big rocks on the lakeshore. You were sizing up the possibility of acquiring a few to paint flowers on. Do you have a black thumb instead of a green one by any chance?"

"I refuse to notice or reply to that remark. Just because I happen to think a rock-flower garden would be easier to take care of than real flower beds . . ."

"Can't say I disagree with you there."

Leonie closed her mouth before she could say more. When they were children, Zara's flower beds and vegetable patches won prizes while Leonie's imitated overgrown lawns. The problem, she now realized, lay in the amount of attention flowers and vegetables required. She didn't mind pitching a baseball over and over again to perfect her style, but overseeing a garden required more patience than she had.

"Here we are." Adam zipped his Jeep into an empty spot at the old school building that housed their class. "Do you think we'll be allowed to touch anything but black paint today?"

"Are you telling me you intend to pick up a paintbrush?"

"I'd just like to see something brighter than black paint sitting on our table, angel."

"I'll see if I can borrow one of the teacher's sample pieces. Maybe that one with the violets on it." She reached back for Butch's leash.

"On second thought, let's just wait and see what she's got in store for us today."

Leonie turned to face the street and froze. "Adam, that bronze car that followed us yesterday just went by."

"I wonder why they haven't changed cars." Adam followed her gaze and they both watched the bronze rental car vanish over a rise in the road. "That's the first thing they teach you in spook school. Change cars, change clothes, change your looks, change everything, and change it regularly."

"I don't like being followed," she grumbled. "I'm going to complain to somebody."

Adam turned back, frowning. "Maybe they're trying to scare you for some reason. Let's go inside before they come back. If they keep on following us, I'm going to alert the police."

Leonie found this statement tremendously comforting. As far as she was concerned, Adam could report that car to the police at once.

Inside the crafts mall, she and Butch settled beside Adam at the table they had used before. "Look. We've got green paint and black paint. I'll bet we're going to paint leaves today."

Adam regarded the paints and their two black rocks with a grim expression she had not seen before on his face. "If you don't mind, angel, I'm going to go out to the Jeep and make a few calls. I don't like you being tailed by this pair of bozos."

"They haven't done anything but follow me," she began and halted.

"I'd like to take them out before they decide to try something else." Adam rose, sliding his phone from its holder on his belt. "Explain to the instructor that I'll be back in as soon as I've taken care of some business that's come up."

With that, he gave her a swift kiss on her mouth and strode toward the door. She watched him go, comforted that he took the situation so seriously, mingled with some fright for the same reason.

"What do you think, Butch?" she muttered. "Will he ever apply a single dab of paint to that rock of his?"

Butch looked from Adam's disappearing figure back to Leonie. To her amusement, Butch seemed to think he ought to follow Adam.

"You turncoat," she said. "You've been bribed, haven't you? One slice of bacon, and you're his for life. I'll have to fix you a whole meatloaf or something in order to win you back."

Butch, obviously a dog who knew on which side his bread was buttered, regarded her with an expression of such intensity, she wondered if he understood her.

"Never mind," she told the dog. "He'll be back in sooner or later, or he's in serious trouble. He's our ride back to the cabin, and he'd better not forget it."

• • •

Adam sat in his Jeep for almost an hour making and receiving phone calls. He reported the bronze car to the Hot Springs Police Department and received assurances that the police would send someone out to take a statement from him. He also called the park ranger station that had jurisdiction over the public lands at Lake Ouachita and reported the suspicious boaters that he now felt certain were monitoring Leonie's activities. Hopefully, a park ranger checking the boaters' fishing licenses might put a damper on some of the spying.

He called his contacts in Washington, D.C. once more, and the only thing he could learn was that Agent Zara Daniel was on a highly classified mission, and he was not to interfere in any way.

It was most frustrating and left him with the same option he had already chosen; namely, that he was not leaving Leonie's side during the next week or so. However long she stayed at Zara's cabin, he was staying. That meant he needed to know exactly how long she intended to take Zara's place.

He returned to the classroom at last and took his seat beside her, pausing to give Butch's head a rub. "What are you painting?" He could see very well that she had applied green paint in the shape of leaves all over her rock, but he had to open the conversation somehow.

"We've progressed to primrose leaves." She showed him a sheet covered with leaf sketches. "This is the shape of primrose leaves, so you'd better get started if you want to catch up."

"Sure." He made a show of pulling his rock toward him and picking up a paintbrush. "How long are you going to stay at your cabin?"

Instantly, her suspicious blue gaze riveted on his face. "A couple of weeks at least, maybe longer. I'm not quite sure." She thought for a moment. "A lot depends on when my boss gets back. I was told a month, but that's not at all certain. "

"Ah, yes. I'd forgotten about him." He smiled at her. "I just want to know how long I need to make arrangements to stay. My brother usually uses the cabin for a couple of weeks in July, and that's coming up next week."

"Oh." The suspicion faded from her face. "Well, if you have to go back to Dallas, I'll certainly understand."

She had no idea. None at all. Marveling at her obtuseness, he said, "My brother would never dream of chasing me off. He's been after me to spend some time with him and his wife for a couple of years." He studied the leaves she had painted on her rock and added casually, "You'll like them."

Zara had never shown a bit of interest in meeting his relatives, and he had certainly gone out of his way to make sure she never came near the cabin when his relatives were there. He'd have hated to explain Zara to them.

From the look on her face, Leonie had no intention of ever meeting his brother and sister-in-law. "I'm sure I will. The teacher says we'll put the flowers on tomorrow, so you'd better get busy on your leaves."

Adam dipped the tip of his paintbrush into the green paint, thinking hard. From the little she'd said, he gathered she was to impersonate Zara for a month, but if Zara finished her project and returned to the States in less time, Leonie's job would end when Zara returned.

For one outraged moment he wondered if Zara would actually try and take Leonie's place in his bed. More to the point, would Leonie let her?

Leonie gave a faint, horrified exclamation. "Adam, that is not a primrose leaf. I don't know what it is, but it doesn't look like a leaf at all. You're ruining your rock."

He glanced down at the big green splotch on a background of black. "It's moss. What's wrong with a moss-covered rock?"

"Moss-covered rocks are a dime-a-dozen out in the woods behind our cabins." She studied him severely. "We're painting primroses on rocks. Now give me that paintbrush and let me try and straighten out this mess."

He gladly sat back and watched while she turned the splotch into several leaves by using small strokes of black paint. "Thanks, angel. I think I might be a little artistically challenged."

She made a sound indicative of amusement. "How would you know? Have you ever actually tried any kind of art?"

"I'm afraid not," he said meekly. "I could tell it was beyond my modest capabilities the minute I looked at it."

"Then why on earth are you in here?" she demanded. "And don't try and tell me you're in here because I'm in here."

"Okay, I won't."

She looked up and promptly turned fire-truck red. "If you make me ruin this rock, I'm bouncing it off your head."

Adam grinned, well pleased with her reaction. He reminded himself that Leonie Daniel was not accustomed to men going out of their way to get her attention. Very likely Zara had claimed all the male attention during their youth, and Leonie probably thought he was really interested in Zara.

He wondered when she would realize that he wanted Leonie Daniel instead of Zara, and how she would react.

That was a day he looked forward to with great anticipation.

• • •

Leonie had a wonderful day. After she had painted primrose leaves on both their rocks, Adam took her and Butch to a downtown café that boasted outdoor tables, and ordered her a lunch of soup, salad, and sandwiches. Then he drove them back to the Crystal

Shack, followed her around the dozens of crystal-filled tables and shelves inside, and stood beside her as she pondered the huge chunks of crystal-studded quartz lying all over the yard.

"You can forget that one," he said. "It'll never fit in my Jeep."

"Maybe I can have it delivered," she said, tongue in cheek. "It sure would look great by the back deck."

Adam let out his breath on a long-suffering sigh. "They'd have to use a truck. I'll bet delivery would add fifty-dollars to the cost of that thing. What happened to the coffee-table piece you were talking about earlier?"

"I've already picked out—There's that bronze car again." Leonie watched it, narrow-eyed. "This time, I'm getting the license number."

Adam turned to watch the highway. "It was LMP836 this morning."

The car flashed past them, and Leonie strained her eyes to the utmost. "It's not the same car," she said. "The plate reads: QLT484."

"It's the same car," Adam said. "They just changed the plates. It's a common ploy, angel."

Leonie glared after the car, outraged. "They can't do that. It's against the law."

"It is that." Adam grinned at her. "But what's a little change of plates compared with all the other things they probably get away with?"

"Like what?" she asked suspiciously.

"Who knows?" He laid his hand on her waist. "But let's not hang around here. Let's buy your coffee-table display and get back to the cabin."

"Why?" Leonie sucked in her breath. "Do you think they're going to break into my cabin and go through my things?"

"Wouldn't surprise me in the least." Adam kept his gaze on the highway. "Now would be a good time, while you're involved in your class and away for at least a couple of hours. Have you been working on something highly sensitive?"

"I suppose so." She thought a moment on what a secretary to the president of a special interest group would consider highly sensitive. "My boss has always said environmentalists are fanatics who will stop at nothing. I'll bet they're trying to find out what our new talking points are going to be. So they can develop counter-arguments in advance," she added.

"You think the environmentalists have hired spies?" Adam sounded amused.

"Not the environmentalists. Their lobbyists. Believe me, Adam, lobbyists are a different breed. Nothing is too low for a lobbyist to attempt in order to get an edge."

She hoped Adam didn't know any lobbyists. She wondered if Zara knew any and decided she had better tell Zara the tale she had told Adam to explain her spies.

"I had no idea that all this sort of thing went on in the hallowed halls of our government," Adam said, shaking his head sadly.

"I'm going to buy a nanny cam," Leonie grumbled. "Although they've probably got a lot of that high-tech surveillance stuff that detects hidden cameras. If I saw a blanked out portion, I'd at least know somebody had been there."

"In a case like this, the best thing to do is assume somebody has either already been in, or will be in shortly." He followed her inside the shop. "There are other ways to know whether or not anyone has been poking through your things."

Leonie abruptly remembered she was supposed to be Zara, and Zara would know all about ways of detecting snoopers. She cleared her throat and said, "Yes, I know. I'll take a few steps as soon as I get back. This is the one I want. Isn't it beautiful?"

She stopped before a chunk of rock the size of a watermelon with large, perfectly formed quartz crystals standing out like icicles. The more she looked at it the better she liked it, and it would look fantastic in her apartment's small living room. It would also look good in any new apartment she found, assuming she could get a job and pay her rent.

"Isn't that a bit too big for a coffee table?" Adam shoved his hands in his pockets and regarded the piece with what she could only describe as a baleful look.

"Not at all." She signaled the shopkeeper. "Besides, I may place it on a bookshelf or even in a special spot on the floor."

"I'll bet Butch will know what to do with it," Adam said under his breath.

"Butch knows how to conduct himself in cabins and apartments." Leonie waited while the shopkeeper, a middle-aged man with rugged features and the leathery skin of an outdoorsman, easily lifted the big chunk of rock and carried it to the front desk.

She followed him to the desk and produced Zara's credit card. She had all Zara's identification and credit cards, since Zara had claimed she wouldn't need them where she was going, and Leonie might need them if she had to make purchases or if she got pulled over by the police.

She signed the credit slip with Zara's signature, which she had diligently practiced for all of five minutes. It would serve Zara right if she sat around nights wondering what on earth Leonie had charged at the Crystal Shack that cost nearly two-hundred dollars. Leonie considered it a memento of her time at Lake Ouachita, but Zara would probably wonder if she had run mad, even when Leonie paid her back.

Maybe she had run mad, Leonie thought, smiling to herself as she presented Zara's driver's license as identification. She was conducting a red-hot affair with Adam Silverthorne in her sister's name, and she was depleting her already skinny bank account—or, for the moment, Zara's bank account—buying what amounted to a bunch of pretty rocks. There was a lot to be said for living in the moment. She had never enjoyed herself so much in her life.

The man at the counter surveyed her signature, frowning, and Leonie's heart promptly stopped. She berated herself for not practicing the signature more diligently. What would she do if she got caught now, right in the middle of what would, no doubt, rank as the most exciting love affair of her life?

Just when she thought she couldn't stand there another minute, the man glanced between the card and Zara's driver's license and handed her back the card. She glanced surreptitiously at the photograph of Zara on the license experienced a moment of profound thankfulness. For the moment, she really did look exactly like that photograph of Zara, thanks to makeup and hair color.

Adam drove them back to her cabin and carried her new purchase inside for her.

"Why don't you just walk down to the lakeshore and pick up a few rocks there?" he asked. "You're bound to find one just as big and heavy as this one."

"Stop complaining. You can't find a rock covered with big quartz crystals like this one on the lakeshore and you know it. But I am going to look for some nice-sized rocks to paint flowers on." She waited while he set the rock carefully on an opened magazine in the center of Zara's coffee table. "There. Now doesn't that look beautiful?"

"More than beautiful," Adam said.

She looked up and discovered his gaze fixed on her face. "I wouldn't go quite that far," she said, flushing. "But it definitely adds interest to the room. Tomorrow I'll have to check out another shop for a few shelf pieces."

Adam strolled over to a bookshelf where Zara kept several big coffee table books and a few bestselling novels, none of which Zara ever read, so far as Leonie could tell.

"As a matter of interest, if you fill up all your available space with quartz crystals, where are you going to put all the flower-painted rocks you're intending to add?" He stood looking intently at the bookshelf.

"All over the place," Leonie said happily. "Rocks with flowers painted on them look good almost anyplace, including outside on the patio."

She could hardly wait to get to roses, the subject of the following day's class. Her primroses, to her delighted eye, filled the place of a flower garden nicely and they didn't have to be cultivated or watered or talked to.

"You'd better check your bedroom drawers." Adam's voice turned grim suddenly. "Someone has gone through these books, and you can bet whoever it was has also gone through everything in your bedroom."

"They went through all the books?" Leonie couldn't believe it. "What on earth do they think I'm hiding there? For their information, I don't have anything of interest to them anywhere in this cabin."

"People hide all kinds of things in books, angel." Adam bent to pluck a coffee table book off the shelf and smiled at her. "Like money." He opened the book and showed her a twenty-dollar bill lying between the pages. "I put this here yesterday. Whoever tossed the room left it alone, but he disturbed the other indicators I left in place."

"You booby-trapped the bookshelves?" Leonie knew now she had entered an alternate universe. "This sounds like some kind of bad spy novel. Why would—? Never mind. I probably don't want to know." She reluctantly withdrew her mind from contemplating roses on rocks and directed it toward checking her belongings in her bedroom. "I wish I had thought to booby-trap my drawers. Maybe with a rat trap or two."

"That would have been interesting." Adam followed her into the bedroom. "We might have come home to find someone hanging off your dresser."

It wasn't funny, Leonie thought, as Adam watched her carefully go through everything in her bedroom drawers. This kind of thing definitely dampened a woman's enthusiasm for vacations. It even made her jumpy and suspicious.

"I'm sorry, Adam," she said at last. "I can't tell if anyone has been through my things or not. Everything looks just the way I left it."

"They've been here," Adam said. His positive tone left no doubt about the matter. "They're just trolling for any information they can find right now. The important thing is whether or not anything is missing."

Leonie truthfully had no idea. "Not that I can tell. But if I think of something, I'll tell you right away."

"Good."

Adam stretched out his hand to touch her hair. To her surprise, he plucked a long, silvery strand of her hair and held it before her eyes.

"Now I'm going to show you a simple way to discover whether or not someone has been going through your things," he said and smiled into her eyes. "But first, I've spent far too long looking at rocks and crystals. It's time I feasted my eyes on something a lot more interesting."

"And what would that be?" Leonie asked innocently, even though she read the message in his eyes very clearly.

"Take off all your clothes and I'll tell you," he said.

"Is this a new form of show-and-tell?"

"It's more like show-and-demonstrate."

Leonie had no fault to find with that program.

"Okay," she said. "So long as it's educational."

Chapter 10

Adam ambled back to his cabin, where he intended to pack a change of clothing and a few of the food items he had stocked for his stay. Overhead, the stars twinkled down on him. Lights and fires from campsites around the lake glittered through the trees, and the moon was full and bright enough to light his path. He didn't need to resort to the tiny but powerful flashlight he carried in his pocket.

He made his way along the wooded trail contemplating why the spooks were snooping through Leonie's belongings, while he automatically noted every sound and movement along the path as he'd been trained to do. Though he'd left the agency five years ago, some of the old habits remained strong.

He wondered if Leonie knew he had once worked in a job similar to Zara's. More to the point, would it make a difference if she did?

Even though Leonie firmly refused to discuss the future and seemed unlikely to ever tell him on her own that she wasn't Zara, he thought he finally had a line on what was going on in that enchanting brain of hers. She thought he was some sort of summer fling. It would have angered him if he hadn't realized she thought he was conducting the fling with Zara. The problem was that he had no idea how to tell her this fling had a long way to go without resorting to telling her he knew she wasn't Zara.

He still wanted her to be the one to confess the truth first, even though he realized her loyalty to Zara would likely prevent that.

It was ridiculous. Why it was so important to him, he had no idea. When it came down to it, what difference did it make whether she thought he was making love to her or to her sister, so long as he was making love to her?

But it did matter on some deeper level Adam shied away from exploring. He accepted that it mattered and went back to his immediate problem, that of convincing her to trust him enough to let him into her life.

He stepped out of the woods and into the landscaped clearing that marked his brother's cabin, only to discover all the lights blazing. He had left only one light glowing in the big family room.

All his senses went on alert. Adam remained in the shadow of the trees and stared toward the cabin. Then he caught the gleam of reflected lights off the polished finish of a silver SUV parked in the spot where he usually parked his old Jeep and relaxed. Seconds later, a man came out on the cabin-length deck and looked toward the darkness of the woods.

"Adam? Are you out there?" It was his brother, Jeremy.

Adam started forward, surprised. "I wasn't expecting you. What brings you here in the middle of a merger?"

Jeremy's computer engineering corporation had just bought a languishing computer showroom in Little Rock. He and his board of directors had been spending twelve and sixteen hour days thrashing out the details of the buyout. According to a newspaper article Adam had read the day before, the thrashing out process was nowhere near completed.

"Mom, of course." Jeremy strolled forward as if unaware he'd just dropped a bombshell on Adam's head. "I came to warn you. She's on her way. Scent of a woman, or some such thing."

"*What?*"

Adam applied a few choice epithets to himself. He should have known he was in for trouble. His mother had called that morning and left a voicemail to check on how his vacation was progressing, and he had yet to return the call.

He hopped up the wooden steps and joined his brother on the wooden deck.

"She seems to think," Jeremy said, wrapping one arm around his brother's shoulders, "that you've finally met the woman you're going to marry. Care to tell me what this is all about?"

"Sounds like you know more than I do," Adam said, returning the hug with one of his own. "Are you telling me you left your negotiations to check out my marital intentions?"

"Maureen needed a break, and frankly, so did I. So we decided to pack it in and head for the lake when Mom called. The negotiations are temporarily stalled, but if your love life has finally gotten into high gear . . ."

"Forget it." Adam thought of graceful ways to skip off to Hot Springs and rent himself a hotel room. "No such luck."

"No woman? Not even the scent of one?" Jeremy sounded amused.

Adam studied his older brother's face in the half-light cast by the inside lamps and reminded himself that Jeremy had already been through this. Perhaps he had some advice to offer.

He drew in a deep breath of the pine-scented summer night air and let the loud singing of frogs and crickets soothe the unaccustomed nerves that assaulted him suddenly.

"The scent of a woman is about all there is at the moment," Adam revealed. "How Mom got wind of her, I don't want to know because I swear I didn't say anything."

"That's why they call it feminine intuition." Jeremy kept his arm across his brother's shoulders. "She's agonized over you ever since Deborah Mills dumped you for that lawyer ten years back. Thought it drove you into taking all those foreign assignments and kept you from finding yourself a promising young wife, now that you're home for good."

Adam stood at the deck rail and stared blindly toward the woods. Ten years ago, he'd thought his heart was broken and that all women were as mercenary and as false as Deborah Mills. He had accepted the job with the agency because it promised travel, and at that moment, he wanted badly to get out of the United States.

Somewhere along the way, he'd regained his faith and enjoyment in life.

Since meeting Leonie, he realized he had also regained his faith in women. Even if Leonie never told him the truth about her identity, he still intended to marry her.

The thought was so surprising, Adam couldn't help grinning. "Mom is either seriously psychic, or she doesn't have enough going on in her life since you and I left the fold."

"Mom never has so much going on in her life that she can't worry over us," Jeremy said dryly. "Seriously, Adam, I thought you were out here writing the proposal that'll put your firm in the black for years to come. Are you sure you've got time to court a woman?"

Adam started to say he wasn't courting a woman, but had to shut his mouth on the words. Chances were that was exactly what he was doing.

"I finished drafting my proposal yesterday," he said at last. "And I need a vacation. That's why I'm here. But if you and Maureen want the cabin to yourselves—"

"Don't be stupid," Jeremy interrupted then laughed. "And don't use us as an excuse to hide out in some hotel in Hot Springs. I'd be forced to tell Mom the name of the hotel."

"Traitor." Adam resigned himself to a cabin filled with his family for the next few days and turned his mind to ways of being with Leonie in spite of his relatives' presence. "When's Mom arriving?"

Beside him, Jeremy froze. His hand gripped Adam's shoulder, directing his brother's attention to something on the edge of the woods. The crickets and frogs sang on, undisturbed.

"There's someone out there," Jeremy said softly. "Do you think your girlfriend followed you back here?"

Adam stiffened but managed to lean casually against the deck rail. He turned just as casually to direct Jeremy's attention toward the trail that led to the lake, all senses on the alert. While he did so, his trained gaze scanned the dark, wooded area Jeremy indicated.

For a long moment, nothing moved, but as he and Jeremy continued to scan the woods while discussing a possible motorboat ride the following morning, Adam became aware of a slight movement in the deeper shadows. Whoever had followed him was trying to vanish, unnoticed, back into the woods.

Suddenly furious, Adam leaped over the deck and raced toward the woods. If he could just get a glimpse of the person who was terrorizing Leonie . . . .

Sounds behind him indicated Jeremy followed. But even as he entered the woods and swept his little flashlight out of his pocket, he knew it was too late. Crashing noises ahead indicated the watcher had decided to quit while he was able.

Adam realized he was an idiot, chasing someone who might turn out to be armed and dangerous. Moreover, he was dragging his brother into possible danger. Courting Leonie had affected his mind.

He jogged to a halt. At least, he had put a scare into the person spying on them.

"What now?" Jeremy said from beside him, barely audible over the crickets and frogs singing their nightly serenades.

"We'd better go back. Maureen won't like it if both of us vanish without a word and leave her alone."

Jeremy turned and walked beside him through the loud, fragrant night air. When they reached the deck stairs, he halted and turned to face his brother. "Do you care to tell me what this is all about?"

Adam sighed. "It's a long story. Why don't you comfort yourself with the thought that, this time, it isn't me they're interested in."

There was a moment of silence then Jeremy's hand clamped down hard on Adam's shoulder.

"If you think that comforts me, I'll take you down to soak your head in the lake," Jeremy warned.

"You can try." Adam laughed, suddenly feeling better. "And keep your mouth shut. I don't want this getting back to . . . anyone."

Even in the darkness, Adam could see his brother's grin. "Oh, I wouldn't think of spreading this around to anyone who goes by the name of *Mom*. Go ahead, brother. Talk."

For once, Adam was happy to comply with an order from his older brother.

• • •

Leonie awakened after a night spent dozing and tossing and long-ing for Adam's presence. She glared at the sun. She did not want to get out of bed. She so did not want to go to her rock-painting class.

She told herself firmly she also did not ever want to see Adam Silverthorne again. He had called her the night before and gave her a long explanation about his brother's arrival, but something about the whole scenario rang false in Leonie's ears. Most likely Adam had decided that one night with her was enough. The fling was over. He probably intended to avoid her, or maybe even escape back to Dallas.

Well, let him, she told herself. A vacation romance was, by definition, limited anyway. Why drag things out?

She felt like crying. Then she got mad and told herself she could not possibly be in love with a man she hadn't even known a week. She ought to go for a good long swim and forget the rock-painting class, at least for one day.

But Leonie was a creature of duty. Having paid her money, she wasn't about to miss a single one of her classes if she could help it, Adam Silverthorne or no. If she treated him coolly, perhaps he'd get the message and leave her alone.

If he showed up at the class that morning—a mighty big "if" in her opinion.

She wasn't holding her breath on that one. The only paint he had applied to a rock so far was that awful green splotch she'd spent time correcting yesterday.

To make matters worse, the telephone rang the moment she finished her morning shower.

"All right, baby," Zara said. "Confess. What was Adam Silverthorne doing over there?"

Baby. That was a big-sisterism designed to keep her in her place. Leonie reflected that she was twenty-six years old now and didn't have to report to Zara about her private business. The best defense was a good attack.

"You tell me," she said in her huffiest tones. "He's supposed to be your boyfriend and he's driving me crazy. If you don't do something about him right away, I'm going to tell Mama everything, and she'll tell Daddy. Shame on you, Zara Daniel."

"Shame on *me*?" Zara sounded absolutely flabbergasted. "What are you talking about?"

"I'm talking about the things you and this Adam Silverthorne have been doing together, that's what I'm talking about. You're supposed to be setting a good example for me, but let me tell you something. Mama's going to have a lot to say about the kind of example you're setting. First, there's this excuse for a bathing suit of yours."

She was on a roll, Leonie thought. Poor Zara didn't know what she was defending against, or where the next blow was coming from.

"No wonder he thinks I'm a—a bimbo," Leonie flowed on. "And those cookies he bakes. They're absolutely sinful. I'll bet I've gained five pounds."

Leonie wished she hadn't mentioned the cookies, but it was too late now.

"More cookies?" Zara exclaimed, outraged. "Leonie Daniel, if you don't tell me what's going on this minute, I'm sacking this mission and coming home to sort this out myself."

"And I'll tell you another thing," Leonie ranted, enjoying herself hugely. "I don't appreciate being followed by those two goons in the bronze sedan. It's getting on my nerves. What if they're serial killers or rapists? I want you to call them off right now. Do you hear me?"

The conversation went downhill from there. By the time Zara gave up and ended the call, Leonie very nearly breathed fire.

"That'll keep her busy," she told Butch. "Do you know, I just realized something. If I'm suffering from little-sister syndrome, poor Zara probably has a huge case of big-sister syndrome. I never realized before how maddening it must be to always have to set a good example for your little sister."

For some reason, that thought sent her into a fit of giggles. By the time she and Butch stepped out the front door of the cabin for their morning swim, she was in a relatively good mood despite her troubled night and Adam's continued absence.

"I know what I'm going to do after we finish painting our roses," she said to Butch. "I'm heading to the nearest department store and buying a decent bathing suit."

"Butch and I both say we like the one you're wearing," Adam said.

Leonie whirled. Adam came toward her around the side of the cabin.

"Well, I don't." She regarded him in a challenging way. "I'm scared I'm going to fall out of it."

"I'll catch you, angel," he said, grinning. "Ready for a good swim?"

"I thought you said your relatives were in. Aren't they going to wonder why you disappeared?"

"I told them there was a good-looking woman staying in the cabin behind us who expected me for an early morning swim. They understood."

"I'll bet." But her spirits soared. This was not a good omen for her future peace of mind.

He reached her and pulled her against him for a lingering kiss. "Believe me, when they get a look at you, they'll understand even more."

Leonie hoped they never got a look at her. The less acting she had to do, the better, and it went very much against the grain with her to deceive Adam's family, not to mention Adam.

But that was between Adam and Zara, she told herself righteously. She was just a stand-in for Zara, and chances were that Adam would tire of the affair and head back to Dallas long before Zara's mission ended.

But he was here now, and that was what counted. She gave herself to the kiss, melting into his embrace with embarrassing eagerness.

Adam lifted his head and stared at her. "I have an even better idea. Let's adjourn to your bedroom for a marathon session of sex."

She wanted to so badly, she almost gave in.

But not quite. "If you're going to feed me home-baked cookies, I'm going to have to swim. It's that simple." She broke loose from his hold and headed for the lake before she gave into the longing that swept through her at his mere touch.

"Slow down, angel. I've been up most of the night, and it's a little tough keeping up with you this morning." He and Butch paced along beside her.

"Good. I ought to be able to beat you to the outcrop and back." She did not intend to ask him why he had been up most of the night.

"Were you born cruel, or does it come naturally?" He glanced down at Butch. "Does she treat you this way? I'll bet she didn't even save me any breakfast."

"Breakfast was served at six," she said. "Butch ate your share of the pecan pancakes."

"Pecan pancakes?" Adam actually groaned. "This is what I get for standing guard outside your cabin all night? No pecan pancakes?"

"Actually, it was French toast," Leonie admitted. "Why were you standing guard outside my cabin? Or should I be scared to ask?"

"Some goon followed me to my cabin when I left you last night, and I caught sight of him. So I figured I'd better keep an eye on your place in case he returned." Adam tossed his shirt to the ground and stepped out of his trousers to reveal a pair of bathing trunks beneath his clothes. "My brother helped. He had a great time, by the way, and he sends you his thanks for an exciting evening."

Leonie heard this with trepidation. "I'll bet he does. And I'll bet his poor wife would like to break a frying pan over my head. Come on, Adam. Nobody likes to be around somebody who's being trailed by spooks and peeping Toms."

"My family loves the exciting life," he said, grinning. "They can't wait to meet you."

Leonie grimaced. "I'm sure. Let them get over the shock for about a week before you plan on introducing me to them. The introduction will probably go a lot better."

She stepped into the water quickly and paddled out into deeper water before Adam saw the truth in her face—that she had no intentions of ever meeting his family if she had anything to say about it.

"You'll like them." Adam caught up to her. "They already like you."

"How can they? They've never met me." She struck out for the outcrop that marked her daily distance. "Maybe you'd better give the painting class a miss. I'll explain to Mrs. Phelps that you've got family visiting."

"Not me." Adam's swimming didn't appear to be affected by his sleepless night. "I can't wait to paint primroses or whatever it is we're painting today. Wouldn't want to get behind."

Now she knew he was teasing her. "That's right. After the roses, we're doing tulips, and after the tulips, there are daffodils or lupines. Who knows. If you miss the roses, she might not let you touch tulips."

"That would be punishment indeed."

Adam stayed right beside her, obviously full of vim, vigor, and male vitality that would have annoyed her if she hadn't longed to make love with him so much. She couldn't out-swim him, so she contented herself with concentrating hard on her technique. One had to stay in shape and remember all the basics, just in case. Her next job might include coaching a swim team.

The moment they arrived back at their starting point and came onshore where Butch sat with dignity beside their belongings, Adam swept her up in his arms.

"Now I'm going to finish up what I never got to start last night," he said.

Leonie was so far gone, she couldn't think of a single thing to say that would stop him. Not that anything would, she thought, on an intense wave of gratitude for that fact. Adam tended to be really single-minded when sex was involved.

In spite of the time spent making love and cooking Adam several slices of her specialty French toast, they arrived at Leonie's rock-painting class in plenty of time. With no bronze car shadowing them, she spent an enjoyable morning mastering the art of painting a rose on a single, smallish rock.

Adam watched her, smiling, and even deigned to pick up a paintbrush himself. He painted the background color on his rock and gave it to her for the painting of the flower.

"Prepping them is well within my capabilities, but I always flunked anything involving creativity," he said.

Leonie thought she had never been happier in her life. She had discovered an agreeable hobby, her surroundings were stunning, and she had a handsome, tireless lover for what she considered the ultimate vacation romance. Could life get any better?

She should not have asked.

"By the way," Adam said, as he boosted her into his Jeep. "We're meeting my brother for lunch at the Mountainside Manor."

Leonie froze. "What?"

"My brother and his wife are buying us lunch." Adam studied her face and broke into laughter. "I never turn down a free lunch, angel. Don't look so scared. Unlike Butch, they don't bite."

In the back seat, Butch heard his name and turned his long muzzle toward them.

"Butch doesn't bite," Leonie said automatically, while her mind turned over this new development. "Look, Adam, I'm not dressed for lunch at a nice restaurant. You'd better drop me off at that store on—"

"I'm not leaving you alone in some store," Adam said. "Not while those two goons are tailing you."

"They're not tailing me today." Leonie set her jaw. "Besides, they can't very well abduct me out of a store full of people, especially with Butch looking after me."

"Nothing against Butch, darling, but I'd rather look after you myself." Adam, still grinning, came around and hopped up beside her. "Besides, they're dying to meet you."

That was what Leonie was afraid of. She searched her brain but could not find one single excuse that would cause Adam to take her back to her cabin.

Fortunately, she had chosen to wear Zara's shocking pink silk blouse—one that left her arms and part of her chest bare—with a tried-and-true pair of her own jeans. Zara would have chosen a pair of skintight white toreador pants, but Leonie figured the blouse was enough of a shock. The color reflected a healthy glow onto her skin and cheered her up just gazing at it. She would just have to bluff her way through the lunch and try to think like Zara.

But it was going to be a really long and stressful lunch.

•••

The two men, now driving a white rental car, followed them at a distance, careful to keep a car or two between them and the Jeep.

"Are you sure this is going to work?"

"Positive," Bolt said. "She'll come after him, never fear."

"You'd better be right." Lloyd stared balefully out the windshield at the Jeep, a small, dark dot climbing a small mountain peak. "So far, the dog goes where she goes."

"They've got to be going to Mountainside Manor. It's the only thing on this road past this point. The dog will have to stay outside in the car."

"You hope."

"It's the law," Bolt said blandly. "Animals aren't allowed in restaurants. For once, the law is on our side."

Chapter 11

Leonie watched the rolling, tree-covered mountains and said little as Adam guided the Jeep straight up the narrow highway, until she realized the restaurant was cut into the side of the mountain near the top. "It looks like it's going to fall off the mountain."

"No chance of that." Adam leaped out and came around to help her step down. "The view from the dining room is fantastic. You'll love it."

When Adam took her arm and led her toward a table, she was so mesmerized by the spectacular view of Hot Springs far below the mountain, she didn't immediately realize the table was occupied by three people rather than the two he had mentioned.

Adam brought her back to earth abruptly.

"I'd like you to meet my mother, angel," he said, "Frances Silverthorne. And this is my brother, Jeremy, and his wife, Maureen."

Leonie gulped. For one brief instant, her surroundings whirled around her. How, she asked herself, through the roaring in her ears, would Zara handle this one?

With finesse, of course. That was how Zara handled everything—as if she knew exactly what was going on, which Leonie didn't, most of the time.

"I'm so pleased to meet you," she said in what she knew were thin, fading tones, and somehow managed to mitigate her voice by turning on a warm smile. "I'm Zara Daniel. Don't we have a wonderful view of the city from here?"

"Wonderful," Jeremy agreed, casting a meaningful glance at Adam as he stood to shake her hand.

Jeremy Silverthorne looked like an older version of Adam, with the same green eyes and dark hair. Maureen, his wife, was a striking brunette whose brown eyes reflected a sharp intelligence and sense of humor.

Frances Silverthorne retained the dignified beauty and peaceful gaze of one who had been the cherished wife of a successful man. Leonie recognized the look because her own mother had it in spades. She was a woman Leonie would love to converse with—under almost any other circumstances.

At the moment, however, the only thought rampaging through her brain was that she was deceiving them all, including Adam. She felt like a liar and a thief. None of Zara's lectures about serving her country could mitigate her deception.

Adam seated her then took the chair beside her, smiling warmly at her. While she pretended to concentrate on the menu, Adam's relatives teased him about his old Jeep and its effect on her hair.

Great. That meant her hair probably looked like a tornado-struck haystack.

"I'm so happy to know you, Miss Daniel." Adam's mother probably had no idea she had successfully frozen Leonie's very blood. "What a beautiful blouse you're wearing. You must tell me where you found it."

Leonie almost swallowed her tongue. Where did Zara do most of her shopping? She had no idea, even though Zara had told her in great detail about the exclusive boutiques she patronized.

"Oh. My blouse." She looked down at it and wished she'd worn almost anything else. Moreover, her fingers itched to throw Zara's silver windbreaker over her bare shoulders. With Adam's mother, in a blue knit dress and matching jacket, gazing kindly at her, Leonie felt dreadfully underdressed. Un-dressed was more like it. "Well, I definitely remember buying the jeans at J.C. Penney."

Zara was going to kill her, Leonie thought miserably. Zara eschewed J.C. Penney and any other store that wasn't an exclusive boutique full of the sexy, flashy clothing she favored.

Maureen and Frances both laughed with understanding.

"I'll bet you bought that blouse and a dozen other things at the same time," Maureen said. "Adam says you live in Houston. Do you shop at the Galleria?"

Leonie nearly fainted. She had slipped, and badly. True, she lived in Houston, but Zara lived in Washington, D.C. She should have followed her first instincts and avoided Adam Silverthorne from the very beginning. Enjoying herself with him, she had forgotten her cover story and had somehow released the fact that she lived in Houston.

Operatives, Zara would lecture, couldn't afford to forget their cover stories. That kind of slip cost good agents their lives every day.

"I have shopped at the Galleria," she said, with perfect truth. "It's one of my favorite places. My sister lives in Houston, and she's taken me around when I've visited." She hastened to change the subject. "But I think this blouse came from a boutique in New York. Do you live in Dallas, Mrs. Silverthorne?"

"Call me Frances, dear. I live in Little Rock, but I do spend a lot of time in Dallas."

"Keeping an eye on Adam," Jeremy supplied, grinning. "No telling what he'd get up to if she didn't watch him."

"When she isn't keeping an eye on you," Maureen said to Jeremy. "She's promised to come to us next week and show me how to brew that special nerve tea you like so much. Maybe that'll help get you through this merger alive."

Leonie smiled dutifully and tried not to let herself get sucked into believing she was a member of the Silverthorne family. That was the way they treated her, and to Leonie, nothing could have been more seductive. Although she appreciated the love and acceptance they projected toward her, she couldn't kid herself into believing it was all for her.

She was Zara, not Leonie. They responded to Zara's all-embracing charm. She had to remember that.

"What do you do, Miss Daniel?" Frances asked. "Adam said something about—" She caught Adam's eye and broke off. "I'm sorry to say I've already forgotten what he told me."

Leonie chanced a look at him, but Adam's face bore no identifiable expression. Perhaps Frances had memory problems.

"Please call me Zara. I'm basically an executive secretary," she said with as much of Zara's zest as she could manage. "My boss is head of a political action committee that represents the fertilizer industry. It's exciting work, complete with a weird schedule and eccentric employees, located in the most dynamic city in the country. What else can a woman ask for?"

"No traffic and a job that makes a difference to the lives of young people, that's what else," Maureen said, chuckling. "That's what I asked for, and that's what I got."

Leonie came to attention.

Rightly interpreting Leonie's involuntary show of interest, Maureen smiled with understanding. "That's right. Since I don't have children of my own yet, I decided to adopt about a hundred of them. I teach chemistry and earth science at our local high school."

Leonie exhaled slowly so she wouldn't blurt out the fact that she was a teacher herself, and for many of the same reasons.

"We're very proud of Maureen," Frances Silverthorne said with a warm glance at her daughter-in-law. "I was a teacher, too. My subject was high school algebra."

"That sounds so interesting," Leonie said, careful not to reveal the full extent of her interest. "Teenagers fascinate me, perhaps because they're at that age where they're forming habits that will stay with them all their lives."

"Perfectly true," Maureen said. "Lots of them will never know any more science than what they learn in high school."

Leonie considered her words, decided she'd better shut up while she was ahead, then spoke anyway. "I've always thought how much fun it would be teaching teenagers how exercise and diet can change their lives for the better, but—"

"You, too?" Maureen looked delighted. "I'm going to be teaching two health classes next semester. Maybe you know some good books."

Leonie knew exactly what books to suggest and was full of pointers developed on the job. Fortunately, she caught Jeremy's curious gaze before she could launch into the subject properly.

"I'm afraid not," she managed. "So far, it's just a dream."

So far as Leonie was concerned, the lunch went downhill after that, even though Adam's relatives put on a good show of enjoying her company. She had to stay on her toes to avoid saying anything that would reveal her identity. Worse, Adam's family pushed every button she had in their discussion of teaching as a career.

She found it amazing that Adam's brother's wife and his mother were both teachers. Leonie couldn't have prayed for better—if Adam had been truly hers instead of Zara's. If she believed for one minute that Adam was serious about her, rather than just wanting a brief vacation affair with a woman who knew the score.

On that note, she ordered a steak and a green salad. She needed the protein to keep her feel-good neurotransmitters in heavy production. She had a feeling she was going to need them if she was going to give a good performance as Adam's vacation girlfriend to his family.

Leonie scolded herself. She was getting ahead of the situation, thinking this lunch had anything at all to do with Zara's relationship with Adam. According to Zara, the cabin Adam was staying at belonged to his brother, Jeremy. That meant Jeremy and Maureen were in Hot Springs to enjoy their cabin, not to meet some girlfriend of Adam's.

Frances Silverthorne clearly was a welcome visitor at any time. Both her sons adored her. Probably, she was simply paying a motherly visit to her sons at a time when she could catch them both together at Jeremy's lakeside cabin.

So why, Leonie wondered, did she persist in believing Frances had come here especially to check her out as a possible bride for Adam?

• • •

Adam decided the lunch wasn't nearly as grueling as it could have been, even though Maureen's slip had nearly caused Leonie to blurt out the truth about her job. He could almost see her every thought as she considered how best to answer every question his relatives posed after that.

How he was going to explain this little question-and-answer session to Leonie was another matter. It was perfectly obvious to him that his mother was assessing her suitability as a member of the Silverthorne family. He hated to imagine what Leonie thought of the third degree his family put her through.

Not that his mother and Maureen weren't perfectly polite in their questions. It was his own fault for telling them the truth about Leonie's masquerade, and that she taught physical education for the Houston Independent School District. He knew they wanted badly to feel Leonie out about her pedagogy and her teaching philosophy.

Worse, Leonie was dying to tell them. He was rapidly becoming aware that she had strong beliefs on the subject of teaching physical education, and she had at last located an interested audience, one that understood exactly what she was talking about.

"I think," Leonie announced, "that there's nothing more important than getting the idea across to kids these days that if they eat nothing but fast foods, they can't expect any brain function to speak of, and they're dashing their hopes of getting into Harvard or Yale."

"That bad?" Adam asked, remembering the many pizzas and hamburgers he had consumed during college.

"Worse." Leonie leaned forward, radiant with enthusiasm. "And the hardest thing is getting it across to these young beauty queens that eating a solid, high-protein breakfast is the first step toward maintaining a normal weight for the rest of their lives."

Adam watched her, enchanted anew. If he'd thought she was stunning before, she absolutely glowed with energy and passion. Why hadn't he realized how she felt about her job?

Because she was pretending to be Zara, he reminded himself. Zara was very different from her sister.

He'd never seen anything like it. Leonie actually *loved* teaching teenagers about the connection between their bodies and their minds. He had been right. Leonie was passionate about everything she did, including her work.

"You are so right." Maureen slapped the table lightly with her palm. "My ten o'clock classes always resound with under-the-desk crackling from candy bar wrappers."

"Ten's the time their blood sugar really hits the skids from eating no breakfast," Leonie said, nodding. "No wonder grade school children are so much at risk for Type II diabetes these days."

"They need to take the candy and soft drink machines out of the schools," Maureen declared.

"They'll just sneak junk food into their lockers," Jeremy said. "You can't legislate what a kid's going to eat anymore than you can tell him what to think."

"Do you remember how we never used to be hungry until noon because our mothers made us eat eggs and bacon and biscuits for breakfast?" Leonie was clearly in her element. "The public school systems need more mothers like that."

"My feelings exactly," Frances chimed in. "That's why I stopped teaching when I had my boys. I didn't go back until they were in high school, and even then, I made sure the family ate a good breakfast together every morning."

"Even if she had to get up at five," Jeremy added.

"Because breakfast was the only meal we ate together," Adam finished. "Jeremy and I had football practice and track after school. Plus, Dad worked late a lot, and Mom tutored some of her more challenged students."

"One thing about teaching physical education is that you don't have to tutor anyone after school." Leonie smiled blandly. "Unless, of course, it's track season, basketball season, or volleyball season. Or swimming season. Or soccer season. "

Frances and Maureen laughed appreciatively.

Adam frowned. If he wasn't mistaken, that little statement meant Leonie didn't have much time for a life of her own. Furthermore, judging from the tone of her voice, she liked it that way.

Well, he'd just see about that. She was going to make time for him. Adam tuned out temporarily while he mentally arranged flight schedules between Dallas and Houston, and thought about long weekends spent in Leonie's company.

"I know exactly what you mean," Frances said. "My family complained because I was always staying late at the school for tutoring sessions. They were all spoiled, of course. Then, there were the nights the Math Club met . . . ."

"And the Junior Anachronism Society," Maureen added in dry tones. "Fortunately, Jeremy has been so busy with the business, he hasn't noticed all the weird costumes in the guest bedroom."

"I thought you were making new curtains," Jeremy said. "Are you telling me those were actually costumes?"

By the time Adam tuned back into the conversation, the others were deep in a discussion of the computer industry as applied to the public school systems. Leonie thought all the emphasis on computerized learning was ridiculous as the children were sedentary enough already, whereas Jeremy was firmly in favor of placing a laptop or tablet computer on every desk.

"Of course, he sells them," Maureen said. "And there has to be some way of making sure children without access to computers at home learn something about them."

"Even the poor kids have smart phones." Leonie looked accusingly at the smart phone on Jeremy's belt. "At the most, they need maybe one or two classes where they concentrate on the basic operations of a computer. Everything I read says more and more computing tasks are migrating to tablets and smart phones anyway. That means the kids know more than the teachers when it comes to tech."

"Maybe the schools need to buy more computers because computer games are better babysitters than television," Adam offered.

Across the table, Jeremy shook his head, laughing. Adam grinned back. He didn't have to be a computer genius to know Leonie would jump on him over that one.

She did, blue eyes flashing, and raked him over the coals thoroughly for daring to use either a television or a computer as a babysitter. In her opinion, he needed to give maybe one or two talks on security analysis in some local schools and get a look at some of the results of electronic babysitters for himself.

He hadn't enjoyed a family lunch that much in a long time, Adam reflected while watching Jeremy pay the bill. What was more, his family loved Leonie and showed their satisfaction by inviting her to the cabin that night for a family supper on the deck. They closed around her in the windowed foyer of the restaurant and said they would not take no for an answer.

Leonie, clearly torn, remained firm in declining the invitation. She claimed her boss had emailed her some research that needed completing before the following morning. If Adam hadn't already told his relatives the truth about Leonie's masquerade, they might have blown everything by refusing to let her off the hook.

Adam, surprised at his own desire to see her dining at his brother's cabin that night, smoothed his hand over her shoulder, savoring her warmth and softness. "You've got to eat, angel. And it's only a minute's walk—"

"I'll probably heat a can of soup so I won't procrastinate any longer."

She moved away from him slightly, with a frozen expression on her lovely face. He figured she had probably just realized how thoroughly she had given herself away, assuming anyone suspected she was not Zara.

"That doesn't sound good at all, especially compared to my mother's fresh fried bass," Adam said.

She looked up at that. "Fresh bass? Who's catching the fresh bass?"

"Jeremy, I hope." He laughed, mesmerized by the gleaming blue of her eyes and the long, feathery lashes, and moved closer.

"He means Maureen," Jeremy said. "She's far better at fishing than I am."

"You need to play hooky from your boss and come fishing with us," Maureen said. "There's nothing more relaxing and invigorating when you're all worn out from work."

"Then it's settled," Frances said. "All you young people can go catch the main dish for our supper while I putter around the kitchen and get all the side dishes ready."

Adam laid his arm casually around Leonie's shoulders. "You heard the boss. It's your job to help provide sustenance for the family. And enjoy another day of your vacation. You can always tell your boss you weren't in when the instructions arrived."

"He already knows I received them," Leonie said.

If he hadn't been watching her so closely, he might have missed the sudden look of longing that passed swiftly across her expressive face. She liked his family and she wanted badly to join them for supper. But she was probably scared of giving herself away, or, more likely, of creating problems for Zara when Zara returned to retake her own identity.

Now that was a thought. Leonie had created her own place in his heart, and very likely in his family's heart, too. No way in creation could Zara take the place that was Leonie's.

He stared out the wide picture windows at the rolling green Ouachita mountains and wondered what Leonie would say if he proposed to her then and there.

That led to a swift consideration of how he would address his proposal. Did he call her Leonie, or should he call her Zara just to see what she would do?

Probably, she would faint if he called her Leonie. Or assume he was proposing to Zara if he called her Zara. Maybe she would even accept in Zara's name, then skip out and leave him to the real Zara when she returned.

He decided to keep his mouth shut a little longer. One way or another, he intended to marry Leonie, but they needed to get Zara out of the way first.

He walked beside her out of the restaurant, still thinking on the matter while his relatives worked on Leonie about the afternoon's entertainment and the fried fish supper they would eat, provided she did her share and contributed a fish or two.

Leonie looked wistful and said nothing until they reached the parking lot.

"I don't see Butch," she said and headed toward Adam's Jeep, which he parked in a shady spot beneath two tall pine trees.

"He's probably napping on the front seat." Adam said.

"Is Butch the collie you found?" Maureen looked eagerly toward the Jeep. "I can't wait to meet him. Adam says he's very intelligent."

"I didn't find him. Butch found me." Leonie hastened forward. "Butch? Where are you?"

Adam developed a bad feeling when Leonie reached his Jeep, scanned the inside swiftly and even bent to look under it.

"Adam, he isn't here," she said, looking frantic. "He's never taken off before. Something's happened."

"Calm down, angel." He reached her side and put his arm around her shoulders in a comforting gesture. "Chances are he saw a deer or something and followed it—"

"I hear him barking," Leonie broke in. "Listen."

The others reached them and Adam held up his hand for silence. Sure enough, he heard, in the forested area to the side, a series of barks and growls.

"Are you sure that's Butch?" he asked.

Before the words were out of his mouth, Leonie broke from his light hold and raced toward the woods.

Adam ran after her. "Come back here, Leonie Daniel. You aren't going in there by yourself."

She never slowed down, and if she noticed his use of her real name, she gave no sign. She raced toward the shadowed pine forest.

Adam, followed by his entire family, ran after her.

Chapter 12

Leonie leaped off the asphalt parking lot and onto the grass that bordered the cool pine forest. Beneath her feet she noted the cushioning effect of a thick mat of grass and pine needles and remembered to watch her footing, especially while wearing Zara's delicate gold sandals.

She heard the revving of a car engine, then a screech of tires on gravel. A nondescript white car broke from a hidden stretch of graveled road, careened onto the asphalt and raced toward her. Loud barking came from within the car.

"Butch!" Leonie yelled.

She took a few running steps toward the car. When she reached it, the door swung open and Butch leaped out. Before she could react, a man sprang from the car, grabbed her and dragged her into the car, yelling, "Step on it!"

Shocked, she hung half out of the car for a moment with her feet scraping the ground as the vehicle bucked forward. Butch bounded toward her, barking wildly, as her abductor hauled her inside and slammed the door shut. The car took off in a squeal of gravel and grass. Leonie tumbled onto the floorboard facedown and stayed there because of a heavy foot pressing into her back and holding her in place.

Leonie couldn't process events. She was being kidnapped, and neither Butch nor Adam could help her. Terror screamed along her nerve endings, even though she fought to control her breathing as she had learned throughout her years of competing.

This was like a track race, she told herself firmly. She needed to breathe slowly and strive for a relaxed awareness so she could seize her opportunities when they came.

Road noise whistled in her ears and the carpet of the floorboard scraped the tender skin of her right cheek. With a man's heavy leg and arm pressing her down, she could hardly breathe, much less move, but she managed to beat back the terror and tried to think.

What would Zara do in a situation like this? She thought hard and creatively, but nothing occurred to her that didn't involve foresight in the form of hiding a weapon somewhere on her body.

Surely, Adam had seen what happened. He would be right behind them.

But what if he had not seen her abducted? Or the abductors' car had managed to elude pursuit?

Leonie realized she had better not count on being rescued. She would have to await her chance and do something on her own. And it would not be what Zara would do, because she had no clue what a trained agent would do.

The car never slowed down so far as she could tell, and they must have hit every jaw-rattling pothole in the highway as the car careened along. She had no idea even which way they were traveling. Moreover, the longer she lay on the floorboard in a twisted position, the more numb her arms and legs became. When the time came for action, she hoped she remained physically capable.

Moving very, very slowly, she managed to turn her head enough so she could peer up through the curtain of her own hair. The man holding her down was obscured by the hair, but she spotted the gun in his hand easily enough. He kept the barrel trained on her.

"Step on it, Bolt," her captor hissed. "They're getting too close."

"This baby won't go any faster," the driver returned. "We don't need a ticket on top of everything else."

Leonie thrilled to the knowledge that Adam followed close behind them and wondered why the men cared about a speeding ticket at a time like this.

"The guy in the Jeep is gaining," the man with his foot on her back said. "Let's lose him on the turnoff up ahead."

Leonie had no idea where the turnoff was or whether they traveled uphill or down. She didn't know anything other than that she was in deep, deep trouble unless Adam in his Jeep managed to catch up to them. If he did, then she needed to escape so she could rejoin Adam. At least, she needed to give him a chance to avoid being shot.

At the moment, she saw only one way of doing that, and that was to imitate Butch. She gathered herself, tensing all her muscles then relaxing them the way she had once done when preparing for track or swimming races.

"You move and you're dead," the man said. "You're our ticket out of here, baby."

Leonie thought better of saying she wasn't his baby. She made no sound and no movement.

"Stay still and don't try anything. Speed it up, Bolt."

Accordingly, she waited without making any signs of a struggle. Perhaps she could lull her kidnappers into believing she was too scared to make a move. Which she was, more or less.

What had Zara been up to that would make people so eager to get their hands on her? More to the point, what did they intend to do with Zara once they got her?

Leonie didn't know, but as she lay there fighting off terror, she knew only that she did not like any of the answers that presented themselves to her racing mind.

• • •

Adam ran after the speeding car as it bounced over the ground toward the parking lot entrance. Butch, barking wildly, darted forward also. But before either of them could get anywhere close to Leonie, her legs disappeared into the careening car and the door slammed. The car sped toward the highway and turned in the direction of Hot Springs with a roar of its motor and a screech of tires.

"Let's follow them." Adam motioned to Butch and hoped the dog understood. "Come on."

Adam opened the Jeep's door and Butch leaped onto the front seat. He jumped in beside the dog and slammed the door.

"We'll follow you. You might need some help." Jeremy herded his mother and his wife toward his SUV and called, "I can see why you chose the security business. Lots of excitement. Nothing like this ever happens in computer sales."

"It doesn't usually happen in the security consulting business either." Adam started the engine. "Stay behind me. They're probably armed."

He concentrated on his driving as he accelerated onto the highway in the direction the white car had taken. His anxiety rose as he drove, but if he went any faster, the Jeep might fly off the winding mountain road.

Butch whined and kept his long muzzle pointed forward, almost as if he knew Leonie was in the car they were chasing. Adam broke his grim concentration on the narrow, twisting highway ahead to look at him.

"Don't worry, Butch. We'll get her back. I don't think—What the hell?"

They approached a fork in the highway ahead, where the major highway led into Hot Springs and the other turned into a heavily forested area. The white car chose the road through the forest, but before it could complete the turn off, another car, an older model navy-blue Buick, approached the intersection from the direction of the forest and positioned itself to block both lanes.

The white car wavered then dodged around the Buick, clipping the front end. To Adam's surprise, the Buick executed a swift backup-and-turn maneuver and followed closely behind the white car.

"I don't know who they are," Adam said aloud, "but they don't seem to be friends of those two."

He glanced at the mountainous forest, broken in some areas by fenced fields and side roads. They seemed to be heading steadily higher, as if they were climbing one of the mountains. It was hard to tell, thanks to the bushes and trees lining the highway. He managed to gain a little distance, so that he at last had both cars in his view.

The white car took a turnoff on two wheels down an even narrower dirt road. The blue Buick remained on its tail. Adam reached the dirt road and followed the blue Buick, even though he had to peer through a cloud of dirt and dust to do so. He hit a deep rut and the Jeep bounced high in the air and landed with a jolt. Butch slid off the seat onto the floorboard and scrambled back up. Adam hoped the dog didn't bounce out of the Jeep on the next big bump.

The dirt road seemed to travel on forever through the woods where the shrubbery almost scraped the sides of the Jeep, and kept climbing higher. Adam's phone sounded its ring tone. He jolted and reached for it without taking his eyes off the dust cloud obscuring the blue Buick.

"You're still back there?" Adam said surprised to hear his brother's voice. "On this road? You'll tear up your car. I don't how where this road goes."

"There's a ranger station near the top of this mountain," Jeremy said. "The road's a dead end."

"A ranger station? Any chance that a ranger is there right now?"

"Let's hope so," Jeremy answered. "Who are those guys in the blue Buick?"

"I don't know," Adam said grimly. "Let's hope it's not a rival group and we've stepped into the middle of a feud."

He replaced his phone and glanced in the rearview mirror. Jeremy's silver SUV followed at some distance behind the billowing dust his Jeep kicked up. He peered ahead at the cloud of dust they were following and calculated how close they were to the ranger station his brother had mentioned. If the dirt road dead-ended there, near the top of the mountain they were on, it meant that whatever happened next would take place there, whether anyone liked it or not.

He wondered what the two kidnappers had planned. Perhaps they wanted to use Zara as a negotiating tool in hopes of getting some concessions from the U.S. Government.

Or maybe they wanted revenge on Zara. On that thought, his blood ran cold. Telling them they had the wrong woman was not likely to make any difference.

He forced his mind to consider all the possibilities that lay ahead. If the white car tried to double back and pass him on the narrow dirt road, he could stop them. His Jeep was an older model, all metal and sporting a big solid bumper. The mostly fiberglass white rental car would come off a poor second in a contest over who got the right-of-way on the narrow dirt road.

He peered through the overhanging branches and the billows of dust. Ahead, he saw a clearing and a log building that stood near a tall metal tower. The next instant, the Jeep burst into the clearing and he saw that the white car was still in motion, circling the clearing slowly as if seeking an outlet through the encircling trees and brush.

The blue Buick halted and two men leaped out, leaving both doors open. They took shelter behind the opened doors in police fashion, guns drawn and trained on the white car.

Jeremy's SUV bounced into the clearing behind the Jeep, and when Jeremy saw that Adam had halted, he pulled the SUV up beside the Jeep. A moment later, Adam's cell phone sounded.

"What's the plan?" Jeremy asked, when Adam answered.

"There isn't one," Adam said. "Just stay where you are. If you hear gunshots, tell Mom and Maureen to hit the floor and stay there while you get the heck out of here."

"No plan?" Jeremy sounded disappointed. "I thought for sure you'd have something daring worked out by now, where we could save the girl and come off looking like heroes."

Adam wasn't sure whether he should laugh or shake his head in disbelief. "This is what's known as an unprecedented situation. Things are fluid. Very fluid. I don't even know who those guys in the blue Buick are."

"They act like cops," Jeremy said. "Okay. I don't feel quite so dumb now." He paused then added, "This is weird. They're barely moving."

Adam kept his gaze fixed on the white car with its tinted windows on the other side of the clearing. It rolled forward at a very slow speed, but nothing moved inside the car, so far as he could tell. He wondered whether Leonie was sitting where she could see that he had followed her.

Adam had almost forgotten the phone at his ear when Jeremy suddenly spoke. "If you've got guns, I'll take one."

"I don't. You've been watching too much television." Adam stiffened when his narrowed vision caught a movement across the clearing. "The car door's opening. Sit tight. Let's see what goes down."

A short man slowly emerged from the driver's position. Dressed in fishing clothes, he stood still for a moment as if getting his bearings, then produced a white handkerchief from his pocket and waved it.

The two men behind the open doors of the blue Buick remained where they were. One motioned for the driver to move forward, into the center of the clearing.

Adam kept his cell phone at his ear, conscious that Jeremy was also watching the developments.

"What are they doing?" Jeremy asked.

"The white car wants to talk." Adam watched the short man walk toward the center of the clearing and stand near the stairs that led up into the ranger station. "They probably want to trade Leonie for safe passage out of here."

"So what do we do?" Jeremy asked. "Mom wants to go over there and have it out with all of them. Maureen is all for it, needless to say."

"Tell them both to sit still." Adam kept attention focused on the unfolding drama. "I still don't know who the guys in the blue car are." He hesitated. "If anything happens, get the women out of here fast."

"Will do," Jeremy said, with unmitigated good cheer. "But I think the guys in the blue car are cops. I'd better let Maureen drive Mom to safety while I stay to help you."

Adam heard feminine voices disputing this statement while he kept his unwavering attention on developments. The short man walked slowly forward, hands in the air. The men in the blue car remained where they were, in position to shoot, and gave more commands.

The short man shook his head and held out his hands, palms out, in the classical gesture of emptiness.

The rear door of the white car began to open slowly. Adam swiftly stepped down from the Jeep, ready for anything. In another minute, Leonie would emerge . . . .

All hell broke loose. The moment the man in the backseat put one leg out of the car, he screamed and turned to beat at something on the floorboard with one hand while trying to aim a gun with the other. He fell out of the car, and tried to stand up, staggering; Leonie fell out behind him, holding onto his leg with both her hands. He tripped, tumbled to the ground and dropped his gun, still yelling. The gun skidded a few feet away.

Butch leaped out of the Jeep and raced across the clearing to latch onto the man's arm, while Leonie held onto his leg in a choker-hold Adam had never seen before. She sank her teeth into his calf.

The man screamed again. "Let go! Ow! Get them off me!" He kicked at Leonie, but she blocked his kick with her upraised knee.

Adam ignored the two men in the blue Buick. So far as he was concerned, they could have the two crooks in the white car, so long as he got Leonie back. He reached the gun and kicked it further away.

"You can let him go now, darling." He grabbed Leonie's arm and lifted her bodily. "Let go of his leg. Let's let Butch handle this."

"Adam!" she exclaimed. She let go the downed man's leg and reached for him. "Thank goodness you're here."

He wrapped her in his arms and held her close. If she figured she was going to put him through this again, she had another thought coming, and so he would tell her as soon as he got through kissing her.

One of the men from the blue Buick came over to take charge of the man on the ground, and Adam moved her behind him.

"Ma'am, would you mind calling off your dog?" the man asked politely.

"Who are you?" Adam kept Leonie behind him.

"I work for the government," the man said. "Agent Glenn Bieler, sir. I was sent to watch over Miss Daniel once she reported she was being shadowed."

"Fine time for you to show up at last," Adam said. "Who are these goons?"

"That's what we intend to find out," the agent said in grim tones. "Sorry about your scare, Miss Daniel. You were never in any danger. We had a tracer on the car."

Adam found that questionable, but he managed somehow to keep silent. Leonie had probably been frightened enough.

Leonie called softly to Butch. The dog, still gripping the kidnapper's fishing-shirt-clad wrist in his teeth, looked up at her. He gave the wrist one last gnawing with his teeth, then dropped it and rushed toward Leonie. She knelt to receive him and buried her face in his soft fur.

Adam looked down at the kidnapper, who lay on the ground and stared up the barrel of Agent Bieler's semiautomatic pistol. "This is what you get for trying to separate a woman from her dog," he said.

Chapter 13

Leonie buried her face in Butch's fur, filled with gratitude. Butch wasn't hurt, and she was okay. Two government agents had taken charge of the kidnappers. She still had no idea why they had taken her, but she had no doubt Zara's profession was behind the atrocity somehow.

At least Zara had taken her seriously and had sent someone to look after her. She supposed that was something, but this was it so far as Leonie was concerned. She was through being Zara. Let her sister hire an actress next time. Or let her simply go on her mission, with no one to take her place like the rest of the peons in the world.

Her next actions, she realized, included thanking Adam for rushing to save her, and then quietly disappearing, never to be seen again.

Or, at least not to be seen again dressed and made up as Zara. She was through forever with Zara's wardrobe and Zara's identity.

She looked toward the Buick through tear-filled eyes. Both kidnappers sat in the backseat in handcuffs. Adam and Jeremy had gone aside to speak to the two agents, while Maureen and Frances waited in Jeremy's SUV, watching her and Butch. Leonie smiled at them and buried her face in Butch's fur once more. How was she going to get through the rest of the afternoon as Zara?

She was going to tell the Silverthornes the truth, that was how. Then she was vanishing into her cabin and refusing to come out again until Zara got home.

The joy she felt at regaining her freedom turned abruptly into the proverbial dust and ashes. She would likely never see Adam again. Her wonderful summer love affair would end the minute she told Adam who she really was.

She had to tell him, Leonie decided, after a second or two spent following her own thoughts in circles. She couldn't just vanish without giving him a reason. Such an action went against everything she believed in.

Tears filled her eyes. He'd probably be furious. No man liked being deceived the way she had deceived Adam. He'd hate her.

For some reason, that thought devastated her. It was ridiculous, because it was probably better all the way around if Adam hated her. Maybe he would take up again with Zara and suffer no useless guilt.

The real problem, she admitted, was that she loved him. After all the trouble she had gone through to convince herself that she could handle a summer fling, she had gone off the deep end over Adam Silverthorne. Worse, she already loved his family. Was this some sort of judgment on her for her stupidity or what?

Adam left the group near the Buick and knelt beside her, placing a gentle hand on her shoulder. "Are you all right?"

Butch actually turned his long muzzle toward Adam and licked his hand. If Leonie hadn't been so upset, she might have professed herself amazed. Apparently, the dog knew Adam had come to her rescue.

"Yes, thank you." She sniffed back tears. "Butch knows you rescued me and he wants to thank you."

Adam smiled. "Don't cry, darling. I don't think we're going to see or hear from those two again. Agent Bieler says they're recent hires who don't seem to know what they're doing. They told him they were kidnapping you so they could prove to someone called Smith that you were the real Zara Daniel."

Leonie closed her eyes. Once she told Adam who she really was, she never wanted to show her face in the Hot Springs vicinity ever again.

"Everything is going to be okay." Adam wrapped her in his arms and laid his face against hers. "Butch is fine. I won't let either of you out of my sight until I know those two are in prison."

The blue Buick slowly moved around the clearing and headed toward the narrow dirt road that provided the only exit. Both agents lifted their hands to Adam and Leonie, then drove slowly out of the clearing.

Leonie sighed and let herself draw comfort from his strength and warmth. In the meantime, she still had to deal with Jeremy and the two Silverthorne women, who piled out of Jeremy's SUV and hurried toward them.

"Is the dog okay?" Jeremy asked. "He still might get ptomaine poisoning from that goon's arm."

"Are you hurt, dear?" Adam's mother asked Leonie. "There's no need to cry. I feel sure your dog avenged you well on that nasty man. Yes, you're a fine boy. I saw you get that mean old kidnapper."

"Hello, Butch," Maureen said. "You're certainly a smart fellow to help catch those thugs. I'm so glad to meet you at last."

Leonie saw that Butch received the attention with aplomb. He politely sniffed at the hands presented to him for approval and accepted their accolades as his just due.

She, on the other hand, hovered about two inches from total internal meltdown. She felt like a liar, a cheat, and an impostor.

"Adam, darling, you'd better give her your handkerchief. This has all been too stressful for her." Frances patted Leonie's shoulder kindly. "First she has to deal with all of us, then those criminals kidnap her. What a day."

Leonie sniffed harder, determined not to break down. Zara would never burst into tears. It wasn't her style at all.

It wasn't hers either, but somehow everything had spiraled out of her control—if she had ever really been in control. Realizing she loved Adam Silverthorne had undermined any semblance of control she'd had. Now she had morphed into a real basket case, and she couldn't even escape the situation unless she cared to run off and hide in the woods and probably get herself eaten by some dangerous wild animal.

"Th—thank you," she managed. "I'm okay. Or I will be in a minute."

"Too bad I didn't have any guns on me." Adam lifted her to her feet and kept his arms around her. "I could have given one to Jeremy, and we'd have rounded those goons up Old West style."

"What did those nasty men want, Adam?" Frances looked from Leonie, still sniffing back tears, to her son. "What did the agents tell you?"

"Apparently, the goons were in trouble with their handler for spying on a fake and wanted to prove to him that they were following the real Zara Daniel," Adam said and rubbed Leonie's back gently.

"But—" The truth hit Leonie like a baseball bat to her head. "You know I'm not Zara." She turned to stare at Adam's beloved face, unsure whether she should feel outraged or inept and stupid. "How long have you known?"

"Actually, from the first day I saw you." He smiled at her tenderly. "In spite of the obvious physical likeness, you aren't at all like Zara."

"Oh, Adam, I'm so sorry. I told her it wouldn't work." Leonie covered her face with both hands. She felt exposed and ashamed. "It's true I can look almost like her twin, but there's just no way I can carry on like Zara for long."

"Thank God for that," Adam said.

"Never mind, dear," Frances said. "I'm sure you must have done an excellent job, or those two wouldn't have followed you around so assiduously. It's made for some real excitement in the family, let me tell you."

"And how," Jeremy said. "I'm thinking I may have to leave the computer business and apply for a job at that agency where Adam used to work. It really gets the old adrenalin flowing."

"Not until you get this merger over and done with," Maureen said in decided tones. "But I have to admit, I can see the attraction. Chasing after dangerous men on lonely mountain roads can be quite addictive. It was really a lot of fun."

Leonie heard this with a peculiar mixture of embarrassment and relief. They didn't sound as if they disapproved of her masquerade. In fact, they made it sound exciting. She remembered Adam approaching her in church the morning after meeting her in the woods and felt the heat rise in her cheeks.

She regarded Adam with considerable uncertainty and a certain amount of asperity. "No wonder you followed me to church. You decided to have some fun with me, didn't you?"

"Actually, I thought you had followed me." Adam laughed. "If you had been Zara, that's exactly what I expected. But you didn't behave at all like Zara usually did in church. When I discovered Zara had a younger sister named Leonie, it all made sense."

"Rub it in," Leonie muttered, freshly annoyed. She covered her face with her hands once more. "So now everybody knows I'm not Zara," Leonie said. "This is really awful. Zara's going to be so let down."

"Don't be upset, angel." Adam gathered her into his arms and pried her fingers from her eyes. "Nobody else knows you aren't Zara."

"Does anybody else matter?" Leonie asked, despairing. "I was supposed to fool everybody, not to mention anyone spying on Zara's whereabouts, and now everybody of interest knows the truth."

"Look on the bright side," Adam said craftily. "If Zara ever asks you to do this again, you have a perfectly good reason to turn her down."

"I do?" Leonie dropped her hands from her face and looked at him through tears. "You're right. I do. I can't fool anyone, including people who don't even know her."

"It would be better if you just tell her your husband won't let you." Her hands rested on his chest, and he gathered both into one of his. "Because I won't. Too dangerous, not to mention that there's only so much Zara-behavior I can stand."

Leonie processed this statement with a brain that made no sense of anything. "But I'm not married," she wailed, "and I think Zara likes you, so you'd better not say you can't stand her behavior. Oh, this is going from bad to worse. When Zara calls again, what on earth am I going to tell her?"

"I'll talk to her." Adam used his other hand to tilt her chin up to him. "Because there's no way I'm going to marry Zara. I'm going to marry you. As soon as I can. So say yes, so Mom and Maureen can get busy planning the wedding."

"You want to marry *me*?" Leonie stared at him. "But Adam. I'm really not a very exciting person and I don't have an exciting job. Zara—"

"I've got news for you, angel," he whispered in her ear. "Neither do I."

He kissed her thoroughly, taking his time about it, and before she realized it, Leonie was kissing him back.

But she knew she must have misheard everything. Adam surely wasn't planning to marry her. He couldn't be, because Zara—

On the other hand, she had seen no signs that Adam had ever been attracted to Zara. In fact, she got the opposite impression. On that thought, a great joy exploded in her heart. Adam wanted to marry *her*, Leonie. And she wanted to marry him.

"Yes," she whispered, and Adam kissed her again.

"Good," Frances said. "That's settled. Now I can stop worrying about Adam and get on with planning the wedding. You'd better give me your parents' phone number, dear. Your mother will want to be in on things."

"My mother?" Leonie looked at her, still dazed from Adam's kiss. "But—"

"You'll want to break the news to her first, of course," Adam told her. "So you'd better call her the minute we get back to the cabin."

"Break the news? That I'm masquerading as Zara and got caught? Mama would have a heart attack." Leonie frowned and rubbed her forehead. "Zara said I wasn't ever to tell Mama what I was doing. She thinks Zara has a safe office job at the agency, and if she knew I was masquerading as Zara, she'd come unglued."

"She probably already has a very good idea what your sister's job entails," Frances said. "You'd be surprised what mothers know. Besides, you don't need to tell her you were taking Zara's place. That needn't come up at all."

"Really?" Leonie wondered if she had strayed onto the set of someone else's life and remembered that she had. "Maybe you're right. But she's sure to wonder why I'm staying at Zara's cabin when Zara isn't here."

"That's why you're here," Jeremy said, grinning. "Zara's gone and you can be alone."

"You came here to meditate on your teaching philosophy in quiet, natural surroundings," Maureen offered.

"You're now into bird watching and you heard there were sky blue warblers in the vicinity," Adam said, still holding her close.

Obviously, Adam had told his family all about the situation, including her real identity and profession. Leonie's mind slowly adjusted to the new reality, even though standing in Adam's embrace threatened to undermine what little thinking ability she had left.

"Maybe I can go with part of the truth," Leonie said. "I was laid off from my last position, and after searching diligently and getting no results, I retired to the lake to rethink my approach to job hunting."

"That reminds me," Frances said. "I have a friend who's now a principal at one of the high schools in Dallas. I'll speak to her about opportunities for P.E. and health teachers. There's always a big turnover at this time of year."

"I'll speak to the principal at my school," Maureen said. "Don't worry, Leonie. Between us, Mom and I know someone at most of the Dallas schools."

Leonie's head fairly whirled as she grappled with the idea that she had agreed to marry Adam and move to Dallas.

"She can start work in January," Adam said. "She has to get through the honeymoon period first and adjust to living in a new city."

"It'll be pretty hard to adjust to living with you," Maureen said thoughtfully. "Maybe you'd better make it another six months."

Adam laughed and hugged Leonie closer. "Maybe we'll just move into the cabin and live off whatever we can catch in the lake for a year or two."

"That sounds wonderful," Leonie said, and smiled at him. "We can paint rocks and sell them for a living."

"On second thought," Adam said, "maybe we'd better get back to Dallas. I'm a lot better at security consulting than I am at painting rocks."

• • •

"I can't understand it," Zara said, two weeks later as she paced the living room of her cabin. "I leave for one month, and come back to find you about to marry Adam. How on earth could all this happen inside of three weeks?"

Leonie, seated on the sofa with a book of wedding styles open on her lap, bit back a smile. Zara had arrived an hour ago, and she still hadn't gotten over finding Adam at the kitchen table, eating breakfast with Leonie.

"It just did," she said. "What do you think about this dress?"

Zara halted in mid-stride and came to examine the dress. "Not my style. Give me a low-cut gown without a back or sleeves."

"It's for me," Leonie said.

Zara frowned at the pictured frock then studied her sister. "You have a great figure, what with all that swimming and jogging you do. You'd look fantastic in a dress like the one on the next page."

"I'm afraid Mama would have a hissy if I showed up at the church dressed in that." She studied the backless, almost frontless, white satin dress with its deep front slit. "She'd want to know if I was planning on opening a house of ill repute."

Zara collapsed on the sofa beside her, howling with laughter. "You're right, of course. But still, a dress like that, worn with the proper attitude . . . "

"That's the problem." Leonie marked the page with the dress she liked. "I don't have the proper attitude. Which reminds me. You'd better not ever let Mama see you in that bikini you gave me to wear. It's a scandal."

"Yeah." Zara put her hands behind her head and leaned back, stunning in her black tank top and black leather jeans. Not for the first time, Leonie observed that her sister looked like a cross between a helpless Barbie doll and a lethal, but sexy, agent. "She doesn't exactly approve of this outfit either, but that's part of my character. Needless to say, I can't explain that to her."

"You might be surprised." Leonie remembered what Adam's mother had said.

"No, I wouldn't," Zara said. "Seriously, Leonie, what happened? Adam wasn't even giving me the time of day, and all of a sudden, he's in love with you. Believe me, I know the signs. Did he realize you weren't me?"

"He says he knew something was off the first time he saw me." She raised her brows. "I told you I couldn't do your act for any length of time. It's natural to you, but it isn't to me. Then he came and sat beside me in church, and that's when he knew I wasn't you."

Zara rolled her eyes. "That figures. I'll bet you sang all the hymns and listened to the preacher like you always do. No wonder he saw straight through you. Next time, I'll drill you on how to behave—"

"Oh, no, you don't," Leonie interrupted. "Not after this. No telling what could have happened, and all because I was impersonating you."

"Who are you kidding?" Zara asked. "You did great, baby. That wannabe operative is still nursing his leg where you bit him, not to mention his wrist where your dog got him. Agent Bieler said he'd never seen anything like that choke hold you had on that guy's leg."

Butch raised his head to examine Zara, who stared back at him with interest.

"Trust you to adopt the ugliest dog I've ever seen," Zara added. "Although, he will be a lot better looking when his coat grows out."

"Now I know what I'm getting you for your birthday," Leonie said. "A collie puppy—"

"Oh, no, you don't, Leonie Daniel. I'd have to board him every time I left on a mission, not to mention haul him to the vet and remember to feed him." Zara jumped up again. "There's Adam. Does he live here now?" She obviously threw the question out at random, but Leonie's prompt flush made her eyes go wide. "Well, I'll be. You have a lot of nerve talking to me about my clothes, when here you are practically living with a man you aren't married to yet."

"Like you wouldn't do the same thing if you met somebody like Adam." Leonie tossed the magazine aside and hurried to the door to let Adam in. "Come on in, Adam. I've found a dress at last, and Zara says she'll be my maid-of-honor, but only if she can wear black to signify her state of mourning."

Her heart, as always, beat faster the moment she saw him. She still couldn't believe he was hers, or that they were going to be married in another two weeks.

"My mother and yours would probably join forces to stop the wedding," Adam said, smiling at her. He took her hand and glanced at the diamond he had placed on her ring finger several days before. "As it is, they're both agreed that Hot Springs is the perfect place for the wedding. Both our families can get there easily."

"And while we're all here," Zara said, pointing to the coffee table with distaste, "what is this humongous chunk of landscape doing on my coffee table?"

"That's a display piece," Leonie said with dignity. "It's genuine Arkansas quartz crystal—"

"—mined in China or someplace else halfway across the world," Zara said, rolling her eyes again. "She gets these weird fancies, Adam. She adopts ugly dogs, drags home rocks and calls them decorator pieces, and plants flower gardens full of nothing but weeds."

"I know," Adam said. "I would have called off the wedding when I found out about the weedy flower gardens, but fortunately, she's found a cure for that."

"What?" Zara looked from one to the other in disbelief. "Don't hand me that, Adam Silverthorne. You're crazy about her. But I'll bite. Tell me this cure for her famous weed gardens."

"She's promised me an entire patio surrounded by flowers she paints on rocks." Adam pointed to Leonie's small display of rock flowers that lined the window sills. "As soon as she adds a few more flowers, we'll build the patio."

"Oh, please." Zara groaned. "You're both crazy. You'd better plan on buying my cabin, Adam. I'm selling out and buying a place on Lake Tahoe. Arkansas has lost its fascination for me."

Leonie exchanged glances with Adam and said, "Maybe we will. In the meantime, let's talk about that collie puppy I'm going to give you."

Zara tossed back her silver hair and crossed the floor in her high-heeled red sandals with her usual inimitable grace. "Never mind. Although, if you're going to tell me it was Butch who brought you and Adam together, I might have to rethink that."

"It was." Adam put his arm around Leonie's shoulders in a gesture that was both possessive and protective. "He knew me for a rival right away and did his best to chase me off. Fortunately, he was susceptible to bribery."

Butch lifted his head at the mention of his name.

"I knew it," Leonie said. "You bribed my dog. No wonder he's following you around now instead of me."

"Come on, darling," Adam said. "He held out as long as a dog reasonably could."

"True," Leonie said, laughing. "But after you grilled him that steak the other day, he transferred his affections from me to you."

"Butch would never abandon the woman who rescued him from starvation and gave him a good home," Adam said tenderly. "But if we're going to share a home, he has to have some feeling for me, too."

Zara looked from Butch to Adam in thoughtful silence for a moment. "In that case, maybe you'd better buy me that puppy, baby. Obviously, collies know what they're doing when it comes to men."

About The Author

Kathryn Brocato is a lifelong reader and writer of romance who lives with her husband, dogs, and chickens in Southeast Texas. Learn more about her at *www.kathrynbrocato.com*, and visit her Facebook page at *http://www.facebook.com/pages/ Kathryn-Brocato-Author/130436237088005*.

A Sneak Peek from Crimson Romance

(From *The Counterfeit Cowgirl* by Kathryn Brocato)

"Hey, babe, is the rodeo in town?"

The admiring words came from a tall, rangy man in a cowboy hat who lounged against a car parked outside the grocery store. Felicity Clayton tossed an impersonal smile at him. She had been worried that people in Foxe, the small Southeast Texas Gulf Coast town where she'd just arrived, wouldn't take notice of her clothes.

So much for that fear. She'd attracted plenty of notice while shopping in the grocery store and was still attracting attention in the parking lot.

From the slim blue denim skirt that skimmed the tops of her high-heeled cowboy boots to the red bandanna-print shirt, Felicity might have just ridden in off the high-fashion range. Even her hair fit the look. She had pulled the shoulder-length brown mass off her face in deference to the Gulf Coast heat and humidity and fastened it at the nape of her neck with a leather clasp that matched her boots.

A turquoise and silver necklace and ring matched the handcrafted silver belt at her waist, and silver horses dangled from her ears. She completed her eye-catching outfit with a leather purse that resembled a miniature saddle. Her purse held a sheaf of business cards bearing the logo of The Cosmic Cowgirl, the western boutique Felicity owned in Nashville, Tennessee.

"You look … mmm, mmm good, babe," the man added. "A little skinny for my taste, but you sure got class."

Felicity winked at the rumpled pseudo-cowboy. As a slim woman with nondescript brown hair and brown eyes, she figured she needed all the help she could get from stylish clothing. Otherwise, she might fade into brown anonymity.

"Thanks, cowboy," she said and prepared to climb into her shiny, white pickup.

"Buzz off, Leroy," a deep, gravelly voice said.

The voice carried overtones of suppressed anger that attracted Felicity's attention. Whoever it was sounded like Johnny Cash. Turning, she stared at a veritable mountain of a man who was climbing down from a dusty blue truck that had just pulled into the parking lot.

He was over six feet tall, with broad, capable shoulders and thick, dark hair. Felicity didn't blame Leroy for leaving the scene immediately. The new arrival looked madder than a wet bantam rooster.

"He wasn't bothering me, but thanks anyway." Her impersonal smile turned into a mischievous grin when she noted the effect the braces on her teeth appeared to have on him. He winced and closed navy-blue eyes.

She caught her breath. Something about him urged her to put extra energy into her smile.

"I'd like to speak to you a moment, Miss Clayton." He slammed the door of his truck aggressively.

Yes, the man was definitely angry. That and the fact that he knew her name made Felicity doubly wary.

"You have the advantage of knowing my name, Mr … .?"

"Whitaker," he said in a clipped, furious tone. "Aaron Whitaker. Not that it matters. You probably won't be here any longer than it takes to get the money and run."

Felicity's brows lifted in astonishment. "I don't know what you're talking about, Mr. Whitaker. But it's a pleasure to meet you, anyway." She held out her hand.

Felicity was accustomed to a certain amount of hostility from men with fashionable wives who spent a lot of money in her shop. She was always at her friendliest when meeting them. Except that nobody here knew who she was. Perhaps she sold him a piece of farm equipment a few years back when she had traveled the South selling tractors and combines to farmers.

She studied Aaron Whitaker, refusing to let him rattle her. Saleswomen grew impervious to negative reactions, or they didn't stay in sales very long. Besides, without his height and those rugged, tanned features, his contemptuous stare wouldn't have had nearly as much impact. His mouth, a masterpiece of chiseled, stony disapproval, and his square jaw both added to the impression of tough implacability.

She made it impossible for him to ignore her proffered hand. He took it automatically and she noticed his palm was hard with calluses.

She let her gaze glide down him. Weathered, form-fitting jeans hugged his long, muscular legs. He wore scuffed cowboy boots, and a blue work shirt had been rolled up to expose muscular, tanned forearms liberally sprinkled with dark hair.

No wonder he disapproved of her. He was a genuine cowboy fresh off the range, and she was a fashion-house fake. She had never even ridden a horse—at least, not long enough to call it riding. She was all show, whereas this man was the genuine article. Well, too bad. In her line of business, image was everything.

"You favor the cowboy look, I see," she said, and smiled approvingly. "It suits you."

"It doesn't suit you. You look like a rhinestone rodeo queen." He appeared to realize he was still holding her hand and dropped it. "But that's beside the point."

"It's not beside the point if you have any interest at all in fashion." She bared her silver-banded teeth at him. "If I sold men's clothing, I'd offer you a huge salary to advertise for me. You're the perfect example of a working cowboy."

Aaron looked as though he'd just swallowed a huge dose of ipecac syrup. He half shut his eyes, as if the glare from her braces blinded him.

"It's the jeans and the boots," Felicity said helpfully.

"I don't give a damn about fashion." He regarded her with a curious combination of annoyance and dawning respect.

"I see," Felicity said.

A saleswoman had to keep her skills honed. Besides, Aaron's obvious contempt brought out Felicity's besetting sin, the urge to convert people to her point of view. "You favor the man-of-the-earth image. A pair of steel-toed boots—"

"I don't favor any such image," Aaron snapped. "Shut up for a minute, will you?"

Felicity arranged her face into a smile of bland interest. "I'm holding my breath in anticipation, cowboy."

Aaron's expression turned as bland as hers. "You won't be for long. Especially if you're the woman who now owns Lureen Tucker's house."

He threw that out like a challenge. Felicity wondered where Aaron came by his information. She did own Lureen Tucker's house and had for the past five years. Far be it from her to enlighten him, she decided, taking in his scornful navy gaze and ruggedly disapproving expression.

"My breath is still on hold." She ignored the trickle of sweat down her back and the damp feel of her heavy denim skirt. Standing in the direct glare of the sun on a humid September afternoon threatened to take the starch out of her, but she wasn't about to let Aaron Whitaker know that. "What does the ownership of a house have to do with anything?"

Aaron flashed his teeth once more. "Ordinarily, neighborliness is something I prize. In your case, however, I'm making an exception."

She had no idea what he meant, although she experienced a sinking feeling when she recollected the large brick, ranch-style house some distance from her own little wood-frame house. Glancing over his shoulder, she reaffirmed the sinking feeling. The blue pickup was the same double-cab truck parked in the wide, circular drive at the house next door to hers.

"A child could easily fall down that hole you call a well in the back yard." He pinned her with an accusing stare. "I expect that nuisance to be properly covered by tomorrow morning, or I'll sue you. Is that clear?"

"I'm sorry to hear that, Mr. Whitaker." She couldn't believe this. "If there's an open well in my backyard, I'll certainly see to covering it."

"See that you do." Aaron gave her a dangerous smile, his eyes glittering. "Mrs. Tucker says you're all business. Not one penny of profit escapes you, according to her. Now that I've seen you for myself, it's obvious where every penny goes."

Suddenly, everything became clear. Felicity sucked in her breath as annoyance replaced her puzzlement.

"I do think first appearances are so important," she purred. "Don't you, Mr. Whitaker?"

The expression on the cowboy's face was priceless.

"In that case," he said, "maybe you'll see to getting your property mowed and having that eyesore of a house painted. Otherwise, people are sure to get an impression of you I'm sure you don't want them to have."

Felicity was dumbfounded. She had arrived in Foxe barely three hours ago, and already she had made an enemy.

Usually, she never made enemies unless she outsold some of the non-producing, entrenched salespeople. Usually, even her enemies liked her. In fact, Felicity was accustomed to being liked because she always took care to make her colleagues in the sales department look good. What was wrong with Aaron?

She forced a nonchalant shrug. "Sorry, Mr. Whitaker. I haven't been in town long enough to fully assess the property and what needs to be done to it. But you can rest assured that by the time I leave here, that property will be in bandbox condition."

She could safely promise him that. Cleaning, repairing, and selling that house was the reason she was spending her first vacation in years in Foxe. Some vacation … barely one day into it, and already the house was causing trouble.

"We'll see," Aaron said, eyes narrowed with dislike. "A woman like you is usually full of promises she can't—or won't—keep."

"A woman like me?" she echoed, baffled. "What—?"

"Just tell me this." Aaron's voice dripped with contempt. "Was Lureen Tucker your grandmother?"

Felicity felt her face flush. "She was. However—"

"How many times did you visit her in the five years she lived here?"

Felicity's mouth opened, but Aaron cut her off. Worse, two other cars had pulled into the parking lot and she sensed the avid interest of the drivers.

"Well, let me tell you something, cowgirl. I have no use for a woman who treats elderly people like throwaways. That old lady might have been a little spooky, but she was still your grandmother. You never visited her once in all the years I've known her. Neither has anyone else in your so-called family. I happen to know her only visitor was an old guy named Fenton Mills."

Felicity opened her mouth again, but for once the Saleswoman of the Year for three years running failed to get a word in edgewise.

"No one in my family wants anything to do with you. Get that house into some kind of decent shape, then kindly get out of our lives and stay out."

"Do you have any knowledge at all of what you're talking about?" Felicity asked, when she recovered her power of speech.

Aaron smiled. The gesture reminded Felicity of a wolf showing its teeth. "That well is an accident waiting to happen, and now that you've been informed of it, you're going to be held responsible if anything happens before you can get it covered. You'd better pray one of my dogs doesn't fall down that thing."

He turned and bounded into his dusty pickup with a single, powerful motion. He backed out swiftly, without squealing his tires, and drove off without so much as a glance in the rear view mirror.

She stared after him. It looked as though establishing herself as a responsible businesswoman and a good neighbor during her brief stay in Foxe was going to be harder than she thought.

Well, she relished a challenge; nothing was any fun if it came too easily. Still, she was unused to being disliked, and dislike was the dominant emotion on Aaron's face when he'd told her to repair the house and stay away from his family. It was amazing how deflated she felt after the small confrontation, even though she knew the truth about Lureen Tucker and he, apparently, didn't.

"Is everything all right?" The tow-headed teen who helped load her groceries earlier, grinned at her. Country music's hottest female star, Becky Lozano, erupted from his earbuds loud enough to be clearly heard as he approached. "Old Aaron looked pretty put out."

"Who is he?" Felicity asked. "He looks like he just rode in off the cattle range."

"He does own about a hundred head of Red Brahmans," the boy said cheerfully. "But you don't make much off them." He nodded at her truck. "He owns the Chevrolet dealership a mile or so down the highway. Maybe he's mad because you're driving a Dodge."

Felicity glanced affectionately at her new white truck. A thick crust of tiny black insects covered the grill and dotted the hood and windshield. "That's probably it. Are you a Becky Lozano fan?"

"You bet I am." The teenager patted the pocket containing his MP3 player. "Every year, I pray they'll get her to sing at the Rice Festival."

"Maybe they will." She had seen the billboard signs advertising this year's Rice Festival when she drove into town. Thankfully, Becky Lozano wouldn't be anywhere near Foxe during the festival.

"The festival's in a couple of weeks, isn't it?" she asked, just to be sure.

"That's right, ma'am. They've got Randy MacElroy as headline entertainer this year."

Felicity grinned. "That should thrill the ladies."

"Yes, ma'am."

Her denim skirt and bandanna-print blouse clung damply to her skin by the time she climbed into her truck and switched on the radio. Becky Lozano's mellow, Kentucky Hills voice reached out, but before the melody could wrap itself around her, Felicity punched the off-button.

Which reminded her; she needed to buy a new cell phone. Hers appeared to have no service in Foxe. Felicity thought about going in search of one and decided against it. She would enjoy the peace and quiet for maybe one more day.

Dozens of the little black flies that covered the hood of her truck floated in the still air. She supposed she'd better get her truck washed—that was another job for tomorrow.

She turned off the highway and drove down the country road to the house, admiring the flat, green pastures and picturesque, grazing cattle. Rice fields and levees bordered with tallow trees formed a patchwork pattern that was unusual to eyes accustomed to green Tennessee hills. The peaceful scene was unexpectedly soothing.

The whole thing with Aaron Whitaker was a misunderstanding, she decided. He was bound to apologize when he discovered the facts, and when she got the problem with the well corrected—assuming there was a problem. Felicity pictured herself accepting Aaron's apology and grew more cheerful as she imagined an abashed expression on those rugged features.

She turned into the shell-covered driveway of her temporary home, bounced across a couple of ruts, and mentally noted to call out a driveway repairman, along with a lawn-care service and a water well covering business.

Glancing next door—which was far enough away to require a pair of binoculars if she wanted to observe details—Felicity scowled at the dusty blue pickup. Then she noticed an unusual air of excitement about the pristine landscape. Aaron himself stood near the neatly trimmed hedge that separated their two properties, frantically calling someone.

Felicity pointedly ignored him but continued to watch the action out of the corner of her eye. A slim young woman repeated Aaron's actions at the other end of the wide, spreading lawn. Perhaps she was Aaron's wife. A third woman, whom Felicity took to be the housekeeper, ran out of the house and toward a sprawling building at the rear of the property.

Felicity climbed out of her truck with keys in one hand, a sack of cleaning supplies balanced on her other arm, and her gaze fixed on the search. No doubt one of Aaron's dogs had gotten loose and taken off for parts unknown. Felicity experienced a twinge of sympathy for the dog, although she told herself it would serve Aaron right to lose a valuable dog—probably a bull terrier or a Rottweiler. Furthermore, he had no right to drag his poor wife out in the afternoon heat to search for his stupid dog. Felicity grew indignant over his thoughtlessness.

Thoughts of the well out back gave her a twinge of fright, but she vanquished that quickly. If she knew Aaron, and she thought she did after that one brief meeting, he had already checked out the well, probably hoping he'd find the dog at the bottom of it so he could sue her.

She held the grocery sack carefully so the rattle of the paper wouldn't interfere with her snooping and tiptoed across the creaking, wooden porch. Whoever heard of naming a dog Pete? Or Joey?

Perhaps Aaron's children had gone missing. But surely he'd have mentioned them instead of his dogs when he told her about her uncovered well. No, Pete and Joey must be Aaron's dogs.

She frowned. Perhaps the dogs were a matched set of schnauzers like the ones she saw at a friend's house last week in Nashville. Their real names were probably something like Joleibenshen's Benckenstein Venerschnitzel. They probably possessed shelves full of dog show trophies and a sheaf of pedigree papers.

Felicity decided she'd been too harsh. The dogs were probably house pets unused to the humid late summer temperatures of the Gulf Coast. She couldn't let two beautiful schnauzers, or whatever kind of dog he had lost, suffer because Aaron Whitaker was a judgmental jerk.

Setting her sack on the porch, Felicity slung her purse over her shoulder and marched across the thick, high grass toward the bordering estate. Aaron glanced up then ignored her. Even at a distance, Felicity saw the scowl marring his darkly tanned brow.

"I'll help you look for them," she said crisply, as soon as she drew within earshot. "When were they last seen?"

"Thanks, but we don't want your help," Aaron said. "Go on back and enjoy your grandmother's life savings."

"What?"

"You heard me." His smile was silky and dangerous—a strange expression on such a ruggedly carved face. "Mrs. Tucker told me how her granddaughter robbed her of her small savings account. That was why she couldn't afford to get that menace of a well covered."

Felicity started to refute that.

"A woman who'd steal from a helpless old lady is worse than a gold digger," he snapped. "Now get out of here. We have better things to do than waste time with the likes of you."

Felicity overcame her desire to do something violent to Aaron's shins. Even in her own stunned condition, she realized he was in a state of strong emotion that had nothing to do with her.

"Now listen, Mr. Whitaker—"

"*You* listen. I want you off my property. If I have to get a court order to keep you off, I'll do it. Now move it."

"The more people who help you look—" she began.

The very idea enraged him. "I don't need any help from the likes of you. Now get your skinny little fanny off my property before I really lose my temper."

Felicity had faced down too many hostile sales prospects in her former career as a traveling saleswoman to be intimidated by an overwrought dog owner. She produced a soothing smile. "Since you're obviously feeling less than reasonable at the moment, I'll just get on home. I'll keep my eye out for them and call you if I see or hear anything."

"Go away," Aaron fairly snarled.

"After all, two schnauzers should be easy to spot."

Aaron stared at her a moment. "Lady, you are one loony little nutcase. Get off my property before I put you on that silly-looking saddle of yours and ride you clean out of town."

Felicity smiled at the vision of herself riding the miniature saddle on her purse. The artisan had assured her it was correct in every detail.

"See you later, Mr. Whitaker. In the meantime, I'll keep an eye out for your dogs."

She turned on her heel and marched back across the thick, almost knee-high grass, ignoring Aaron's frustrated exclamation. She ruined the effect by tripping over a hidden crawfish mound and nearly falling flat on her face.

So much for being neighborly. Felicity reached her front porch once more and took notice of her damp, steamy state. She was only too happy to return to the air-conditioned comfort of her own place—except the air conditioner wasn't working, and the repairman wouldn't arrive until tomorrow. She inserted her key into the lock and wondered why a man desperate to find his dogs was so equally determined not to accept any help from her. It was downright puzzling.

Something was wrong with her key. Felicity pulled it out and gazed at the key tip. It was coated with a sticky, glue-like white substance. Worse, the door was unlocked. Felicity shoved it open with her booted-foot and glared inside. After tangling with Aaron, she felt primed to deal with a burglar.

She saw no one, but then she hadn't expected anyone. She had already discovered the front door lock was unreliable at best. Felicity registered another addition to her list of repairpersons to call and stalked inside.

Dumping her grocery sack and purse unceremoniously onto the welter of old newspapers and magazines littering the sofa, she turned back and studied the offending lock. The peculiar white substance was now oozing from the keyhole.

Pondering the matter, Felicity retrieved two more sacks of cleaning supplies from her truck and another sack full of boxes of large plastic trash bags. She glared across the expanse of grass. Aaron had crossed the road that ran before their houses and was searching the field opposite, where several dozen humped, mahogany-colored cows grazed peacefully.

To the rear of the Whitaker property, the slender dark-headed woman scurried frantically toward the barn and over to the equally distraught housekeeper. The two exchanged helpless gestures that aroused Felicity's sympathy. As soon as she changed her clothes, she was joining in the search whether Aaron liked it or not.

She threaded her way toward the bedroom. Her grandmother had saved every piece of paper that had crossed her path during the past five years and the stacks formed an obstacle course for the unwary.

The telephone shrilled. Felicity grimaced and detoured to the kitchen to answer it. The kitchen cabinets and one drawer stood open, revealing a collection of pans and utensils interspersed with miscellaneous junk.

"Hi, Mama," she said in patient tones. "Of course, I'm all right. What could possibly have happened to me in the two hours since I last talked to you?" She listened a moment. "Because I was at the grocery store buying gallon jugs of Mr. Clean and boxes and boxes of plastic trash bags, that's why. I told you I was going to the store. I'll get a new cell phone tomorrow."

While reassuring her mother that she hadn't been mugged in the grocery store parking lot, Felicity cast her gaze around the kitchen. Had those cabinet doors popped open on their own?

"Yes, Mama. Don't worry. I didn't realize there was no cell coverage for my phone here. I'll buy one tomorrow that has local coverage. In the meantime, this old landline still works fine."

When she hung up the phone, she became aware of a peculiar odor in the house. Sniffing curiously, Felicity arrived at the bedroom door. She didn't remember closing it, and it seemed a little difficult to push open.

The odor strengthened as the door swung open. Felicity stared toward the windows; the dusty window sills bore oval globs of a pearly-white substance. She looked down. An old towel had been rolled up and stuffed into the crack between the door and the floor. The small room was empty, but Felicity remained on the threshold, her scalp prickling. That odor had to be Elmer's Glue. Grandma Lureen had left several large bottles of the stuff scattered around the house.

Felicity studied every detail of the room. Someone had glued her windows shut. Suddenly, she was glad Aaron was nearby ... surely, he'd come to her aid if she screamed.

Emboldened, Felicity stepped into the room. There were squiggly white lines of Elmer's Glue everywhere, as if someone had tried to seal up every crack in the floors or walls.

A muffled sneeze from the closet made her jump violently. She skittered back to the door, heart pounding madly. It took several seconds for Felicity's brain to shift into gear. She laid her hand on the doorknob, pulled open the closet door, and looked into the frightened faces of two small boys armed for battle.

Each child held a saucepan lid in front of him like a shield, and wore the pan as a helmet. The older boy held a long-handled fork in a menacing fashion, while the younger clutched a kitchen fork. Both seemed oddly relieved to see Felicity peering down at them.

Suddenly, it all made sense.

"Hello, Pete. Good afternoon, Joey." She smiled soothingly. "I'm glad the two of you came to pay me a visit, but why are you waiting in the closet?"

The older of the two boys, who couldn't have been more than five, met Felicity's friendly gaze with wide-eyed trust. "We're hiding," he said in a grave little voice.

"Yes, I can see that." Felicity blinked in surprise. "Your—" she wasn't sure whether they were Aaron's children or not, "—relatives are very worried because they can't find you. What are you hiding from?"

"The ghost." The younger boy scrunched closer to his brother. "The ghost might get us."

Great. On top of everything else, the house that was to be her temporary castle was haunted. Felicity sighed and mentally added "exorcist" to the list of repair people she was about to call.

"Welcome to Foxe, Felicity," she said aloud.

In the mood for more Crimson Romance?
Check out *The Rebel's Own* by M.O. Kenyan at
CrimsonRomance.com.

www.ingramcontent.com/pod-product-compliance
Lightning Source LLC
Chambersburg PA
CBHW010639100726
47900CB00011B/2889